W9-CGO-455

TASK FORCE

RECON TEAM ANGEL

The Assault

Task Force

ALSO BY BRIAN FALKNER

The Tomorrow Code

Brain Jack

The Project

TASK FORCE

RECON TEAM ANGEL 2

BRIAN FALKNER

Property Of
Bayport-Blue Point
Public Library

RANDOM HOUSE NEW YORK

This is a work of fiction. Names, characters, places, and incidents either are the product of the author's imagination or are used fictitiously. Any resemblance to actual persons, living or dead, events, or locales is entirely coincidental.

Text copyright © 2012 by Brian Falkner
Jacket art copyright © 2013 by Alan Brooks
Map copyright © 2013 by Jeff Nentrup

All rights reserved. Published in the United States by Random House Children's Books, a division of Random House, Inc., New York. Originally published in paperback in Australia and New Zealand by Walker Books Australia, Newtown, in 2012.

Random House and the colophon are registered trademarks of Random House, Inc.

Symbol art by snoopydoo

Visit us on the Web! randomhouse.com/teens

Educators and librarians, for a variety of teaching tools, visit us at RHTeachersLibrarians.com

Library of Congress Cataloging-in-Publication Data
Falkner, Brian.
Task force / Brian Falkner. — 1st ed.
p. cm. — (Recon Team Angel ; bk. 2)
Summary: The six teens of Recon Team Angel, having spent years mastering alien culture so that they can talk, act, and think like their enemies, now have their target in sight but time is running out to save humanity and themselves.
ISBN 978-0-449-81299-0 (trade) — ISBN 978-0-449-81300-3 (lib. bdg.) —
ISBN 978-0-449-81301-0 (ebook)
[1. Extraterrestrial beings—Fiction. 2. War—Fiction. 3. Undercover operations—Fiction. 4. Adventure and adventurers—Fiction. 5. Australia—Fiction. 6. Science fiction.] I. Title.
PZ7.F1947Tas 2013 [Fic]—dc23 2012038142

Printed in the United States of America

10 9 8 7 6 5 4 3 2 1

First American Edition

Random House Children's Books supports the First Amendment and celebrates the right to read.

For Kym, Roy, and Alyssa

The future belongs to those who believe in the beauty of their dreams.

—Eleanor Roosevelt

MAP OF NEW BZADIA

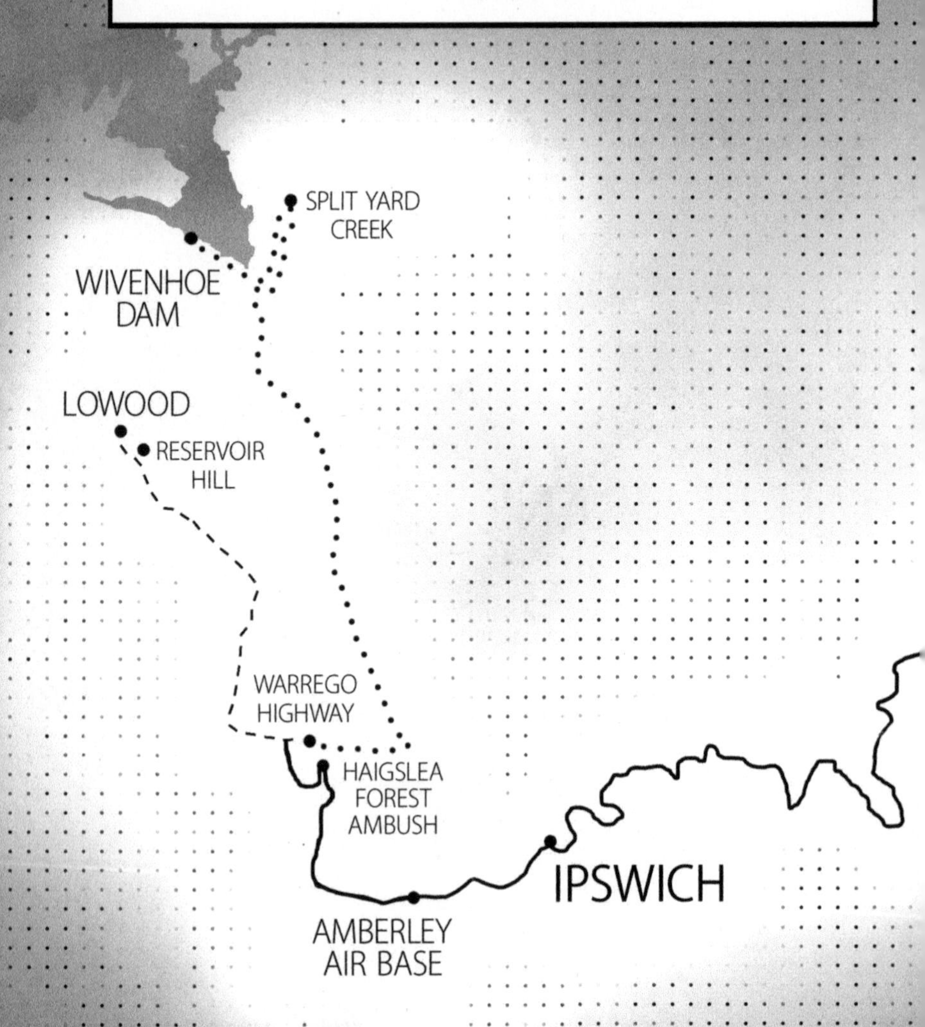

TO
CORAL SEA →
MORETON BAY
ST. HELENA'S
SONRAD STATION
BRISBANE RIVER
COASTAL DEFENSE
COMMAND CENTER
BRISBANE
N
W
E
S

CONTENTS

BOOK 3—THE LAKE

PROLOGUE

THIS IS NOT A HISTORY BOOK.

The achievements of 4th Reconnaissance Team (designation: Angel) of the Allied Combined Operations Group, 1st Reconnaissance Battalion, from November 2030 to July 2035, during the Great Bzadian War, are well documented by scholars and historians. Less well known are the people behind the myth: the brave young men and women who earned the reputation and the citations for which Recon Team Angel became famous.

These are their stories, pieced together from Post-Action Reports and interviews with the surviving members of the team. The stories of the heroes whose skills, daring, and determination changed the course of history.

Where necessary to gain a full understanding of the situations these soldiers faced, accounts have been included from the forces they opposed: from interviews with prisoners and Bzadian reports of the battles.

The members of Recon Team Angel changed over time, due to injury and death, as happens in a combat arena. By the end of the war, over seventy young people had served in the unit. They were aged fourteen to eighteen—small enough to pass themselves off as alien soldiers, but old enough to undertake high-risk covert operations behind enemy lines.

At its peak, this remarkable group boasted a core of twenty-five specialist operatives. But only six "Angels" infiltrated Australia as part of the ill-fated Operation Magnum:

Angel One: Lieutenant Ryan (Lucky) Chisnall—United States of America
Angel Two: Sergeant Trianne (Phantom) Price—New Zealand
Angel Three: Specialist Janos (Monster) Panyoczki—Hungary
Angel Four: Private First Class Blake Wilton—Canada
Angel Five: Specialist Dimitri (The Tsar) Nikolaev—Russia
Angel Six: Specialist Retha Barnard—Germany

May we always remember the names of those who fell in the pursuit of liberty for Earth.

BOOK 1—THE ISLAND

We celebrate our military victories,
but try to forget our failures.
Operation Magnum, however, will never be forgotten.
More than a failure, it was a glorious disaster.
—General Harry Whitehead

1. INVASION FORCE

THE ARMY CAMPED ON THE CHUKCHI PENINSULA IN FAR northeast Russia was the largest assembled in the Bzadian War, poised for the greatest invasion in Earth's history.

The buildup took several months, but by the end of November 2031, there were 7,000 rotorcraft; 5,000 jet aircraft, including 800 of the formidable and heavily armed "Dragons"; 35 tank battalions; and 60 full infantry divisions. Over a million Bzadian soldiers—complete with artillery and logistical support—occupied the inhospitable and frozen wastelands of the peninsula and waited for winter.

Less than a hundred miles away lay Alaska and the pathway to the Americas. As soon as the turbulent waters of the Bering Strait turned to ice, the invasion of the Americas would begin, and with it the beginning of the end of the human race.

On the other side of the strait, human forces also waited. But after seven years of warfare against the mighty Bzadian

Army, Earth's defenses were little more than a thin crust ready to oppose the invasion.

For the aliens, the invasion could not come soon enough. The massive army was a ravenous beast that needed constant feeding. Over 30,000 tons of food and supplies were being trucked into the peninsula each day. Nearly half of that was fuel. The huge battle tanks would use up a fuel cell in two days, the mighty Dragons in just eight hours.

In the Americas, military commanders did what they could to prepare for the coming holocaust. On December 10, representatives from twelve nations—those that still had any significant military capability—met in the war room of the Pentagon to make what plans they could.

General Elisabeth Iniguez, the commandant of the US Marine Corps and a member of the US Joint Chiefs of Staff, was the instigator of what later came to be called Operation Magnum.

General Iniguez, a fiery redhead, stood up and slammed her hand down on the table. "Invade us? Invade us!" she said. "How about we invade them! Those alien freaks."

Her plan was an audacious one, never before attempted. An attack in the heart of the Bzadian Empire, in New Bzadia itself (formerly known as Australia). It called for an amphibious task force to sail down the Brisbane River right under the noses of the aliens. The target was the aliens' fuel-processing plant at Lowood. Without the constant flow of fresh fuel cells, the Bzadian Army would be paralyzed. By the time they could rebuild or repair the plant, the winter would be over and the threat of invasion gone for another year.

The plant was heavily protected by ground-to-air missile batteries, which ruled out an air attack. But an even bigger problem was the Amberley Air Base.

The massive Bzadian air force base located near Ipswich, west of Brisbane, was formerly the largest base of the Royal Australian Air Force and one of only three major air bases in Australia still with its full complement of rotorcraft and fighter jets. All the other bases were operating at lower levels, as their aircraft had been shipped to Russia to support the coming invasion of the Americas. Amberley, and its massed aircraft, had to be taken out of action for the operation to proceed.

General Iniguez knew that everything depended on destroying the air base. If not, then the entire expeditionary force would be wiped out. In her opinion, Operation Magnum was going to be either the biggest triumph of the war or the biggest catastrophe.

As the meeting broke up, General Harry Whitehead, the tall, gray-haired, and soft-spoken supreme commander of ACOG, took Iniguez aside and asked, "Are you sure this can be done?"

Iniguez replied, "I believe so, sir." She looked closely at him and said, "But we'll need Angels on our shoulders."

2. BARRACUDAS

[MISSION DAY 1, DECEMBER 31, 2031]
[1725 hours local time]
[Virginia Class Submarine: USS *JP Morgan*, Coral Sea off the coast of Queensland, Australia]

"BRING HER UP TO SIXTY FEET."

"Sixty feet, aye. Pump from number one auxiliary to sea."

"Very well. Bring her up slowly. Sonar?"

"All clear."

"Showing sixty feet and steady."

"Come to two eight five. Slow ahead both."

"Two eight five, aye. Pump-jets one and two answering slow ahead both."

"Very well. Angel One, this is First Officer Kavanagh. Please confirm your team is ready to Echo Victor."

Inside the lockout trunk, Lieutenant Ryan Chisnall made

an "okay" sign with his thumb and forefinger. The universal diving sign for "all okay." It was both a question and an answer, and the five members of his team responded with matching gestures.

"Angel Team confirmed ready for Echo Victor," Chisnall said.

"Very well. Vent and flood LOT."

"Lockout trunk venting and flooding, aye."

Chisnall pressed his full-face mask firmly to his skin as air hissed out of the chamber and cold seawater rose rapidly around him. There was no need; the mask was well secured. It was just habit.

Lights in the chamber began to dim. The shapes of his five Angel Team members faded into the background, then disappeared completely.

He flicked the night-vision switch on the side of his mask and the interior of the chamber took on an unearthly green glow, his teammates now black ghosts silhouetted against it.

The lockout trunk, a staging area built into the submarine, was for US Navy Seals, allowing them to deploy without the submarine needing to surface. It was designed for nine adults, so for six small teenagers it seemed spacious. Plenty of room for a party. But the six teenagers in this room were not here to party.

"Buddy up and check equipment," Chisnall said as the last of the air hissed out of the chamber. He was now enclosed in a metal box, well below the surface of the ocean, with only his breathing apparatus to save him from a certain, horrible death.

It didn't concern him. Nothing much concerned him nowadays. Not since Uluru.

He turned around so Private First Class Blake Wilton could check his equipment.

Uluru was the first ever Angel mission, and he had been in charge. They had completed the mission and destroyed the secret alien project hidden inside the giant rock in the Australian desert. But the cost had been great, physically and psychologically.

The bulky shape of Specialist Janos "Monster" Panyoczki moved to the much smaller, willowy form of Sergeant Trianne "Phantom" Price, and his hands began moving over the hoses and knobs of her rebreather kit. She pulled away from him briefly, then relaxed, with a quick glance at Chisnall, and allowed Monster to complete the check.

What is up with those two? he wondered.

Specialist Retha Barnard, a stocky fifteen-year-old German, did the checks with Specialist Dimitri "The Tsar" Nikolaev. Barnard's check seemed short and perfunctory, but Chisnall knew it was probably more thorough than those of any of the others in the team.

Barnard and the Tsar, the two newest members of the team, didn't seem to get on particularly well, and Chisnall had buddied them together for that reason. Learning to rely on each other in life-or-death combat situations was a good way to get over petty personal differences.

He had put Monster and Price together for much the same reason. Since Uluru, there had been some kind of tension between them, which both of them denied when he asked about it. But something had changed; Chisnall was sure of it.

A lot of things had changed since Uluru.

Monster had changed. He seemed to have developed a more spiritual side. He was still funny, rude, and rough as guts, but after Uluru he appeared to have started thinking more deeply about things. Most of the conversations Chisnall now had with his friend were on the nature of life and the universe. Chisnall didn't mind. It made for some interesting late-night discussions, and he felt that Monster was just trying to find his way. To figure out his place in the world.

With Brogan gone, the team had needed another medic, and Monster had volunteered for the training. He seemed more interested in helping others than in hurting them, although Chisnall was still confident that he would pull his weight when it came to the fighting.

Brogan. His sergeant on the last mission. But she had been more than that. Much more. Chisnall tried not to think about her. The one person he had absolutely thought he could trust had turned out to be the one person he couldn't. That betrayal had changed something in him, and he didn't like it.

Wilton finished checking Chisnall's equipment and turned around so Chisnall could return the favor. A couple of tubes, a couple of knobs, all were as they should be. But Chisnall already knew that. He had checked it when they had suited up, and then again when they had entered the chamber. He tapped Wilton on the shoulder to let him know he had finished.

Unlike a scuba set, the closed-circuit rebreathers used a

bottle of liquid oxygen with sofnolime cartridges to remove carbon dioxide. With scuba gear, most of the oxygen in the tank was wasted, expelled into the ocean every time the diver exhaled. With the rebreathers, very little was wasted. More important, though, the closed-circuit system eliminated any telltale bubbles on the surface, and the full-face masks allowed for underwater conversations through built-in microphones.

"Equalize pressure."

"Equalizing valves open, ambient sea pressure reached."

"Unlock the hatch. Angel Team is clear to EV."

"Open this tin can up for us, would you, Monster?" Chisnall said.

Monster launched himself up off the deck and braced with one hand on a railing while he spun the wheel that opened the hatch.

The pitch-black of the lockout trunk changed as the hatch door opened, letting in the light of a completely different world: the ocean outside the submarine. It was not bright, just a gentle shimmering of light through the waves, thirty or so feet above them.

Chisnall flicked off his night vision. There was no need for it outside. Not yet.

Monster was first out and waited by the hatch for the rest of the team to emerge before spinning the wheel again to close it.

"Angel Team is EV. Unlocking stowage lockers." The first officer's voice was in his ear again.

The submarine was a long gray tube, smooth as oilskin,

stretching away into the murk of the water behind them. There was a strange beauty to the symmetry of the vessel, broken only by the sail, the squat tower that jutted from the hull of the submarine close to the nose.

Price was first to the sail, where the stowage lockers were located, and she opened the flat panels to allow Angel Team to access the equipment stored inside. The first three compartments held barracuda DPVs, diver propulsion vehicles. Price reached inside the spacious compartment and pulled the first of them out by its tail. It looked like, and was designed to sound like, a large fish. The best efforts of the best engineers trying to create something nature did effortlessly.

Price passed one to each member of the team before extracting her own.

An equipment pod followed, then a small torpedo-shaped object that she floated gently across to the Tsar. He attached it behind his barracuda. A towed sonar array, it would be their eyes and ears in the dark night of the ocean.

"USS *JP Morgan,* this is Angel One. How copy?" Chisnall said.

"Angel One, this is the USS *JP Morgan*. Clear copy."

"Thanks for the ride, guys. We are Oscar Mike."

"Very well. Goodbye, good luck, and Godspeed."

"Everybody ready?" Chisnall asked. He got quick nods from everyone, except the Tsar, who thumped his chest twice with his fist and said, "Boo-yah, Big Dog, ready to rock 'n' roll."

"Someone forgot to take his medication," Barnard said.

"No fighting, kids, or I'll send you to your room," Chisnall said.

He straddled his barracuda and leaned forward, easing open the throttle and feeling the large tailfin behind him begin to sweep back and forth. He twisted the throttle farther, and with a flick of its tail, the narrow rubberized hull slipped silently through the water.

A week at sea on a Royal Navy destroyer, followed by two days on the submarine. Now it all came down to this. The final stage of their journey back behind enemy lines.

After Uluru, Chisnall had sworn never to return to Australia. He had also sworn he would never again command an Angel mission. Yet here he was.

When they came to him, they said Operation Magnum was their only chance. If this mission failed, then the Americas would fall, and if the Americas fell, then the human race would fall. They told him he was the only one with the experience, with the leadership skills, with . . . They said a lot of things, but Chisnall wondered if what they really thought was that he was the only one stupid enough to go back behind enemy lines on a mission that, any way he looked at it, seemed like a one-way ticket.

Another suicide mission.

3. DEMONS

[1735 hours local time]
[Coral Sea, off the coast of Queensland, Australia]

THE DEMONS PASSED THEM AS THE ANGEL TEAM WAS forming up just to the west of the submarine, which was already backing away through the darkening waters of the Coral Sea. The water was clear enough for Chisnall to see the dark hull of a second submarine retreating in the distance.

A thin voice with a coarse Southern accent came through the earpiece of his comm. "They really must have been scraping the bottom of the barrel for this mission."

Chisnall glanced around. The barracuda overtaking him to his left was identical to his own except for a fiery skull and crossbones hand-painted on the bow, the symbol of the Demons. That was not only totally against regulations, but it was also stupid.

"Are you trying to advertise your presence to the Pukes?" Chisnall asked.

The Demon leader, Varmint (they only used nicknames in the Demon Team), grinned. "If they get close enough to see that, then we're already in a deep steaming pile of turd."

"You gotta be kidding me," Chisnall said.

"If I was in the Angels, I'd try to hide the fact too," Varmint said. He laughed and veered off to join the rest of his team.

Recon Team Demon was the counterpart of Recon Team Angel. They looked the same. ACOG doctors had discolored both teams' skin to a mottled green and yellow, reshaped their skulls with bone extensions, and forked their tongues to look like Bzadians'. But there the similarities ended. While the Angels specialized in information gathering, the Demons were trained in demolition and sabotage. They were based at Fort Rucker in Alabama and had a reputation for being a loud, loose group, with few rules and poor discipline. They were tolerated because they got the job done. You had to be a little crazy to go behind enemy lines and blow stuff up; although, Chisnall reflected, the last time he had been in Australia, that was exactly what he had ended up doing.

"Check your six, LT." Monster's voice sounded on his comm.

Chisnall looked over his shoulder, then up as a shadow slid over him. The gaping mouth of a huge fish was rimmed with a jagged jumble of razor teeth. He felt his skin contract inside his wet suit and eased back on the throttle. A shark, and from the sheer size of it, a great white. He reached around for the shark repellent clipped to his arm, making careful, slow movements so he didn't attract attention.

"Azoh!" Wilton said.

In one of those strange quirks of language, human soldiers had started to borrow the Bzadian exclamation, except in their mouths it became an expletive. It had quickly become the rudest word in the English language. Wilton claimed credit for starting the trend, after Uluru, but Chisnall suspected it went back further and deeper than that.

The great fish cruised past above him, showing no interest, but just to be safe, Chisnall squeezed some shark repellent into the water. It spread rapidly, a soft yellow mist.

"Who peed in pool?" Monster asked.

The shark disappeared into the distance.

"Let's get moving," Chisnall said. "Before it comes back."

"Why you worry, LT?" Monster asked. "Sharks don't eat humans."

"You sure about that?" Price asked.

"He's right," Barnard said. "But the way they find out if you're edible is to bite you and spit you out if they don't like you."

"Let's hope it bites the Demons first," Wilton said. "That would leave a bad taste it its mouth."

"A shark would never bite a Demon," Price said. "They can tell when something is rotten."

Chisnall twisted the throttle again and the barracuda began to move.

There was no propeller on the barracuda, or a motor.

Motors made noise. Propellers made cavitation sounds. And both traveled long distances underwater. The sensitive Bzadian sonar on St. Helena Island would pick them up miles away. So the barracudas were silent. There was only the fish tail, flicking back and forth through alternating magnetic fields. Steering was by smaller fins on each side of the craft. The only sounds the barracuda made were the natural sounds of the ocean. Yet the craft could travel at speeds of up to fifteen knots underwater. Behind the narrow bow of the craft, the controls were similar to those of a motorbike, with a throttle on one side of a steering handle.

Chisnall took his place in the team, just in front of the Tsar, also known as the Hero of Hokkaido. What he had done in Hokkaido, no one knew; the mission was top secret. But it had earned him a medal, a moniker, and a place in Operation Magnum.

The Tsar was Russian. Chisnall found him brash and conceited.

The Tsar told anyone who would listen that he was a direct descendant of Grand Duchess Anastasia Nikolaevna, and thus heir to the throne of Russia. Even if that was true, it meant nothing. Russia was completely occupied by the Bzadians. The Tsar had only narrowly escaped before they sealed off the borders. The rest of his family hadn't been so lucky. They were still trapped behind enemy lines. On the submarine, Wilton had asked the Tsar about his family and been told in no uncertain terms to butt out. It was clearly a sensitive subject.

Ahead of Chisnall was the other new member of the team, Specialist Barnard, an intelligence officer (whatever that meant). Barnard's only expression seemed to be a sullen look of disinterest, as if people were neither interesting enough, nor intelligent enough, to be worth her time. If she had a smile, Chisnall hadn't seen it. He couldn't understand why she had been included on this mission, the most vital of all missions. The Tsar, he understood. He was a "hero." He had a reputation.

Barnard did not. She had no combat experience. She had been an Angel for less than a year. Yet she must have done something to impress the brass back at Fort Carson to have earned a place on this team.

Chisnall checked the time on his wrist computer and called in a status check.

"Angel Two, Oscar Kilo." Price was the first to respond, and the rest of the team followed in order, their voices clear on the comm but with the peculiar muffled sound of speaking inside a very small space.

Chisnall switched his comm to the Demon channel.

"Demon One, this is Angel One. How copy?"

"Hush, everyone, the Angels are singing," Varmint said.

"Ain't it beautiful," another Demon voice said.

"Confirm team status, over," Chisnall said.

"We're so good it hurts," Varmint replied.

Chisnall sighed. "Just logging in, Demon One. We are Oscar Mike en route to Target Alpha, now passing waypoint one."

There was a clearly audible snort on the comm. "Waypoint one? What kept you?" Varmint asked. "Were you afraid of the little fishy?"

Chisnall thought of the jagged teeth of the great white. "It's not a race," he said.

"That's what the loser always says," Varmint said.

Chisnall gritted his teeth and managed to stop himself from saying anything more than "Good luck."

"Luck is for wusses," Varmint said.

St. Helena was a former prison island in Moreton Bay, near the mouth of the Brisbane River. It was a picturesque and historic island with a colorful past and was now home to the primary Bzadian sonar/radar (SONRAD) station for the region.

Sensitive 3-D radar constantly scanned the skies, while the passive sonar sensors of the station were giant ears in the ocean. The cavitation of a propeller, the steady drum of an engine, even the swish of water against a hull—*nothing* could escape their attention.

St. Helena Island was Target Alpha for the Angel Team. The SONRAD station had to be out of action before the task force entered Moreton Bay on their way to the mouth of the Brisbane River.

The assault on St. Helena was the kind of mission that the Angels trained extensively for. In Bzadian uniforms, with their skin, skulls, and tongues modified to look like the aliens', they could travel freely where no other human could.

It wouldn't be easy. The security detail on St. Helena consisted of twenty-four guards on rotation. Every four hours, a new shift of six guards would arrive from the mainland and six guards would leave.

The Angels had to be in place on the island when the new shift arrived, to ambush them and take their place. They had all the right uniforms and security codes. With a little luck, they could walk right in without any alarm being raised.

Meanwhile, the Demons were tasked with destroying the electricity grid that powered most of downtown Brisbane. Operation Magnum depended on stealth. On darkness. There was no way to slip an entire task force through a brightly lit city.

After that, both teams would take on a shepherding role, guarding the task force from unwanted attention as it tried to slip quietly up the Brisbane River to the smaller inland city of Ipswich and the adjacent Amberley Air Base. While the task force extricated itself from the river, the Angel Team would relocate to a forward position to provide reconnaissance on the air base, and the Demon Team would head north, to the great Wivenhoe Dam.

Their missions from then on were classified, and not even Chisnall knew what they were. Officially, the reason for the secrecy was so that if any of his team was captured during the early phases of the operation, they couldn't give away details of the later stages. Privately, he wondered if the real reason was because once in, there was no way out.

The Angels swam in a seemingly random and widespread pattern. Wilton was on point, the frontmost and shallowest of the team. The Tsar, at the rear, towed the sonar array.

The meager light above faded as the day neared its end, and Chisnall switched his night vision on. It gave clarity to the water that didn't normally exist, even in daytime, showing rocky outcroppings rising from the otherwise invisible seafloor many feet below. But at the same time, the night vision caused a curious lack of depth, so objects far away seemed much closer, and objects close by seemed far away. Fish—strange, green mooncreatures in the amplified light—flicked in and out of his vision. The water was full of life, far more than he had been able to see with his naked eye. Small creatures wriggled and jittered in front of his eyes, bizarre ribbonlike fish fluttered away from him, long-legged prawns seemed to walk through the water, and shapeless mollusks simply drifted, pushed out of the way by the bow pressure wave of his barracuda.

They passed waypoint two at around 2200 hours. On schedule. Chisnall's shoulders were sore from bending over the handlebars. He checked the oxygen meter on his rebreather. Still enough for a few more hours. Good.

A loggerhead turtle swam across his path, its legs lazily sweeping the water. Ahead, he could clearly see the shapes of the other Angels, the tails of their crafts whispering back and forth.

A rush of water behind him was followed by a white flash overhead, so close that he could touch it. Chisnall recognized the sleek shape of a great white shark, possibly even the same shark they had seen a few hours earlier. It disappeared to the south.

Perhaps it knew they were not to its liking. Perhaps it wasn't hungry. Or perhaps it was still deciding.

"Spread a little shark repellent," Chisnall said, and squeezed some of his own into the water.

"Holy cow, those guys are quiet," the Tsar said. "I never even heard him coming."

"Maybe someone else should be running the sonar," Barnard said.

"Hey, I may not be perfect," the Tsar said, "but parts of me are excellent."

"Which parts?" Barnard asked. "Not your ears, obviously."

"You want to find out? Come and see me after the show," the Tsar said.

"I'll bring a magnifying glass," Barnard said.

"How much can you really hear on that thing?" Chisnall asked, changing the subject before things turned nasty.

"I can hear Wilton," the Tsar said.

"Me?" Wilton asked.

"I can hear you breathing. You're puffing like a steam engine. The Pukes'll know you're coming before we get past Moreton Island."

"What do you want me to do, stop breathing?" Wilton asked.

"Works for me," Price said. "All in favor say aye."

"Hey, you're funny, not just funny-looking," Wilton said.

"Seriously, Tsar, what else can you hear?" Chisnall asked, now intrigued.

"Well, Big Dog, since you asked, the Demon Team is to the south, slightly ahead of us—"

"You can hear them?" Wilton asked. "I thought these barracudas were supposed to be silent."

"I know what to listen for," the Tsar said. "This is not amateur hour. I've spent hours training my ears so that I . . . Hang on, what was that?"

"What?" Chisnall asked.

"I think Monster farted," the Tsar said.

"Keep wet suit warm!" Monster said.

"Oh, great, fart jokes," Barnard said. "I thought I joined the Angels, not the Demons."

"You wouldn't have passed the Demons' entrance qualifications," Price said. "You're not a skinny, loudmouthed redneck."

"I suppose German girls don't fart," the Tsar said.

"Give me your air hose and I'll see what I can do," Barnard said.

"Is natural thing," Monster said.

"Maybe, but some of us prefer not to make it a topic of discussion," Barnard said.

"When I was ten, I could fart 'Rudolph the Red-Nosed Reindeer,' in tune," Wilton said.

"My point exactly," Barnard said.

"What the hell?" the Tsar hissed.

The comm chatter went dead.

"What is it?" Chisnall asked.

"Active pinging, low-powered," the Tsar said.

"Where is it coming from?" Chisnall asked.

"South," the Tsar said.

"Near the Demon Team?" Chisnall asked.

"It *is* the Demons," the Tsar said. "I know this signature. The frequency and pitch. It's their towed sonar unit."

"What a bunch of amateurs!" Wilton said. "Why would they advertise their presence like that?"

"They wouldn't," Barnard said.

"Maybe it was an accident," Chisnall said. "Maybe they flicked it from passive to active by mistake."

Just once, can't a mission go according to plan?

"You couldn't do that by mistake," the Tsar said.

"Maybe it a signal," Monster said. "Maybe they're in trouble."

"Maybe they're trying to warn us of something," Barnard said.

"Everybody hold up," Chisnall said. "Absolute silence." He could hear the pinging now, faintly reverberating through the water around them.

He flicked to the Demon channel. "Angel One to Demon One." He waited a moment, then tried again. "Angel One to Demon One."

"The pinging's stopped," the Tsar said. "So have the Demons."

"What the hell are they up to?" Price asked.

The cold seawater seemed to close in on them as they waited, motionless, for more news from the delicate ears of the sonar array.

"They're Oscar Mike," the Tsar said at last.

"Why did they stop?" Wilton asked.

"Why did they ping us?" Barnard asked.

"We'll ask them when we see them," Chisnall said. "In the meantime, we are Oscar Mike. We can't afford any delays. Stay extra frosty. If they were trying to warn us of something, I want to be prepared for it."

The seafloor seemed to be angling up now, although it was hard to tell in the glow of the night-vision mask. A large dark mass was looming to Chisnall's right, and with a quick check of the coordinates on his wrist computer, he confirmed that it was Moreton Island at the entrance to the bay. They had made better time than he had expected, no doubt helped by the steady current.

Somewhere to the south would be North Stradbroke Island. Once they passed through the gap between the islands, they would be in Moreton Bay and that much closer to their first target: the SONRAD station on St. Helena Island.

From now on the Bzadians would be seeing them on the sonar scope. Hopefully all they would see were six large fish. They tried not to swim in straight lines but varied their course, veering left and right and occasionally flicking around in a circle, as fish do.

"If we really were fish," Wilton asked, "what kind of fish would you be?"

"You'd be a clown fish," Price said.

"Price would be a piranha," the Tsar said.

"What about Monster?" Monster asked with a short laugh.

"A kraken," Barnard said.

"Kraken? What's that?" Wilton asked.

"Get an education and a haircut," Barnard muttered.

"No more chatter," Chisnall said. "The less noise the better. Focus on the mission."

The seabed was shallower here, not a flat featureless plain but rather a crumpled blanket of valleys and channels, ridged like sand dunes. They kept down in the depressions as much as possible to mask their sounds even more.

"Big Dog, I'm picking up a surface vessel in the bay," the Tsar said.

"What have you got?" Chisnall asked.

"Cavitation, sounds like a twin prop. I think it's a Puke patrol ship."

"What the hell is that doing here?" Barnard asked. "Our intelligence reports show no patrol ships in this area."

"Maybe they knew we were coming," Price said, and Chisnall caught the undertone in her voice. Maybe the mission had been compromised before it had even begun. Like Uluru.

"You think they heard the Demons pinging before?" Chisnall asked.

"I'm sure of it," the Tsar said.

They were all silent, letting the Tsar concentrate on the vague noises coming through his headphones.

"It's turning," he said. "It's getting louder. I think it's coming in this direction."

Another pause.

"Cavitation has increased. It just picked up speed."

4. PATROL SHIP

[2220 hours local time]
[Moreton Bay, New Bzadia]

"HOW FAR AWAY IS IT?" CHISNALL ASKED.

"A few hundred meters, give or take." The sonar had no way of measuring distance, other than by the volume of the sounds. "Cavitation has stopped," the Tsar whispered.

"Where?" Chisnall asked.

"About where I last heard the Demons."

Chisnall could imagine them, motionless in the water, scarcely daring to breathe as the patrol ship closed in on them.

"Active pinging, active pinging!" the Tsar said. "The ship is pinging."

Chisnall could hear that without a sonar array. The high-pitched pulse of sound echoed around him.

"LT, your orders?" Price asked.

Chisnall stared to the south as if he could see the drama unfolding there.

The Tsar yelled, "Underwater explosion!"

Chisnall heard it, too, a distant sonic boom, far away but still powerful enough to vibrate the glass of his mask.

"What the hell was that?" Wilton asked.

"Ultrasound depth charge," Barnard said.

"Azoh!" Wilton said.

"LT?" Price asked.

"Keep moving," Chisnall said. "We don't have time to stop."

"They're in trouble," Barnard said. "We have to do something."

"And jeopardize our mission as well?" Chisnall said. "The Demons will have to look after themselves."

"We're wasting our time if the Demons get caught," Barnard said.

She was right. The task force wouldn't make it a hundred feet up the river if the Demons didn't switch out the lights.

"Okay. You're right. I'll go and check it out," Chisnall said. "Everyone else, stay on task. Sergeant Price has mission command till I get back."

"No, LT, I'll go," Price said.

"I can't risk you," Chisnall said.

"Then send Wilton or . . . Monster," Price said.

"Do your job, Sergeant," Chisnall said. "You're in charge till I get back."

He thought briefly about opening the equipment pod and getting a weapon, but that was not possible underwater, and difficult even floating on the surface. He decided not to. In any case he was just going to have a quick look around; he wasn't planning on getting into a firefight.

"And if you don't come back?" Barnard asked.

Chisnall didn't answer. He was already on his way.

Price watched Chisnall swim off, the black shape of his barracuda disappearing into the strange underwater twilight.

"What the hell was that all about?" Barnard asked.

"What?" Price asked.

"Chisnall racing off to be the hero," Barnard said. "What's he trying to prove?"

"Chisnall doesn't have to prove anything," Price said. "Not to me."

"Or me," Wilton said.

"Boo-yah," Monster said.

"He should have sent someone else," Barnard said.

"He should have sent me," the Tsar said.

"Then who would have operated the sonar?" Price asked. "Listen, I know Chisnall. He's not trying to be a hero. He just doesn't want to risk any of our lives, so he's risking his own."

"He's the team leader," Barnard said. "Doing this, he's risking *all* of our lives."

"You're right. He's the leader, and he has given orders," Price said. "Now shut up and follow them."

There was only one problem with what Barnard had said. She was right.

Price checked the time and made a quick calculation. They should reach St. Helena Island only a few minutes behind schedule. Still in time to intercept the security shift change.

"What if the LT doesn't come back?" the Tsar asked.

"Then you're stuck with me," Price said. "But we proceed with the mission as planned."

"LT will be back," Monster said.

"They call him Lieutenant Lucky," Wilton said. "He's a real lucky dude."

"And if they called him General Motors, would he drink gasoline and fart exhaust fumes?" Barnard asked.

"He's the luckiest person I know," Price said.

"It's not luck," Monster said. "The universe, it turns according to a plan, and Chisnall fits somewhere into that plan. He'll be back."

"Oh, right. Of course. There is a plan to the universe," Barnard said. "Stupid of me. I thought it was a random bunch of stars."

"You believe what you believe. Monster believe what Monster believe," Monster said.

"And you can't argue with irrational beliefs," Barnard said.

"So does the universe have a plan for me?" Wilton asked.

"No," Price said.

"Why not?" Wilton asked.

"Because the universe thinks you're a jerk," Price said. "Now cut the chatter and focus on the mission."

"New Big Dog barks just like the old Big Dog," the Tsar said.

"What did I ever do to the universe?" Wilton asked.

It took Chisnall less than ten minutes to locate the ship. He drifted toward it, no more than a vague motionless black shape hidden behind the bright glare of the underwater searchlights. He was noiseless in the water, with only the occasional swish of his tailfin.

He wondered if he was doing the right thing. He could have let one of the others go. He *should* have let one of the others go. He knew that. And yet somehow he couldn't.

He approached the ship from the stern and let himself float upward until he was just below the surface. A small handheld periscope was fastened inside the front of the barracuda. He undid the rubber clips and raised the scope until the water drained away from the lens and the ship appeared: a green monolith in his night vision.

It was a patrol craft, a sleek, fast machine still painted in the gray of the Australian navy from which it had been appropriated. It looked to be about two hundred feet long, with two radar towers amidships and a Zodiac inflatable in a cradle on the rear deck.

A long taut cable stretched away from the stern, disappearing underwater about ten feet from the boat. A towed sonar array. At this close range, they would have had no problem locating the Demons.

There was activity on the stern near two low platforms with steps leading up to the main deck. Another searchlight scanned the surface of the waters behind the ship, a fiery circle in his night-vision mask. He made sure to stay well out of range.

As he watched, the light fixed on something floating in the water. Two Bzadian soldiers used a long, hooked pole to drag it to the platform. With horror, Chisnall realized that it was a body in a black wet suit. The body stirred a little as they hauled it up the stairs to the deck. The Demon was unconscious, but at least alive.

Other Bzadians were bent over something on the deck, and as he watched, they lifted another Demon—dead or alive, Chisnall couldn't tell—and carried him through an open doorway at the rear of the superstructure. Three more Demons were carried into the cabin. Including the one they had just dragged out of the water, that made five. One was missing, maybe dead on the bottom of the ocean.

Shouted orders came from a small main deck, high on the superstructure, to the rear of the bridge. The searchlights cut off and the Bzadians moved to the front of the ship. Chisnall allowed himself to float closer to the stern.

His mind was racing.

The Demons had been captured or killed.

But it was worse than that. If they realized who the Demons were, they would alert Coastal Defenses. The task force depended on stealth and surprise. Operation Magnum would be over before it had begun.

The only rational thing to do now was to return to his team

and they could slink back to the submarine with their tails between their legs.

The water drained away from her mask as Price lifted her head out of the water for the first time since leaving the submarine. For all the navigation gadgets in the world, she still liked to see for herself where she was. Where she was going.

The lights of Brisbane were a forest of color on the mainland, a few miles due west. In front of that, slightly to the north and much closer, a distinct glow came from an otherwise dark mass that had to be St. Helena Island. They were heading in the right direction, and as best as she could judge, they were not much more than a mile away.

She looked to the south, at the lights of the ship. There had been no word from the Demons since Chisnall had left. And no word from Chisnall.

She did another quick radio check but got only silence.

In the absence of any other orders, in the absence of Chisnall, the only thing to do was carry on. It occurred to her that she might never hear from him again. She might never know what happened to him, or the Demons. But those were thoughts for another time.

Right now there were things to do.

There was a team to lead.

Price pointed her barracuda down, and the lights of the city disappeared above her.

■ ■ ■

It was over. Logic told him that. But emotion wouldn't let him leave. Not yet. A waft of his craft's tail propelled him toward the platform. Watching the back of the boat intently to make sure there were no observers, Chisnall reached out for it.

The ship's engine note changed, escalating into a throaty roar. Turbulence bubbled up around him. The bow of the ship lifted. Chisnall rammed his throttle to full.

He nearly made it. The platform edge was just inches from his fingertips when it started to slip away from him, the gap widening as the ship surged ahead. He leaped off the barracuda, stretching out full length, lunging for a metal rail at the base of the platform. His fingers snagged and then lost it as the boat powered away from him in the dark water.

There was a rushing sound, and Chisnall spun around to see the narrow line of a wire rope cutting through the water behind him. The sonar array! He launched himself sideways, grasping the rope with one hand, then the other. It was wet, and his hands slipped. He managed one large gulp of air before sliding underwater. The water came at him faster and faster as the ship picked up speed. His facemask dislodged and began to fill. He locked his hands around the wire, trying to hang on. His lungs were already starting to burn. Rushing water buffeted his face, and he dared not open his eyes.

Tightening his grip with one hand, he managed to slide his other hand forward a few inches. It immediately slipped back, losing most, but not all, of what he had gained. He slid his other hand along, with no better result. A wave of dizziness flooded over him. But he continued. *Slide a hand forward, slip a little back. Slide the other hand forward, slip a little back.* His mind was empty. Nothing existed except moving one hand, then the other, until at last he could do no more. The pain in his chest was unbearable; his brain was spinning. His mouth opened but instead of water, he inhaled a lungful of pure, sweet sea air.

Chisnall took another breath, but this time got water. Spluttering and choking, he took another frantic gasp and got air. His mind began to focus. He was out of the water just enough so that he was able to catch a breath in the troughs of the waves.

Timing his breaths carefully, he opened his eyes and glanced up at the stern of the ship. It seemed to tower above him, although it was only a few feet away. An easy climb on an obstacle course, dry, with fresh muscles. Here in the rough seas, at the limits of his endurance, it was impossible. He knew beyond a doubt that he could never make it. But he had to try.

Chisnall wrapped his legs around the wire and twisted his ankles together, locking the cold metal between them. Without warning, the boat began to turn, a sharp veer to starboard. The force of it almost wrenched him from the wire, and he screamed in frustration and agony. But it was his salvation. As the boat turned, the wire swung to the right and suddenly the metal stairs that led to the platform were almost within his grasp. The impossible now seemed possible, and that thought gave him renewed energy.

He stretched out a hand, scrabbling at the edge of the short flight of steps. His fingers touched it, then slid away. Again he tried, and this time the waves were kind and the rocking motion of the boat brought the stairs to him. He gripped it with a strength that he didn't know he had. The boat began to straighten. He flopped into the water, his fingers steel claws on the railing of the stairs. He swung his other arm up and now both hands locked on, the rest of his body bouncing over the water behind the ship, buffeted by the turbulence from the propellers below. Two hands became two hands and a knee, then two knees, and finally he collapsed onto the platform.

He could have lain there and gone to sleep, or at least rested until he got some feeling back in his numbed fingers and legs, until the fires that burned in his muscles faded. But there was no time for that.

There were shouts coming from the deck above him. They were hunting again.

Price could hear the pinging through the cool water even before the Tsar spoke. It sounded like the tolling of a high-pitched bell. *A warning bell.*

"Active pinging," the Tsar said. "Cavitation has increased, getting louder. They're coming this way."

"I've got a bad feeling about this," Wilton said.

"Spread out as much as you can, but stay in comm range," Price said. "Head for the island. Barnard, you're supposed to be the intelligence officer. Do you know anything about these depth charges?"

"The ultrasound blast will stun you up to about ninety feet," Barnard said. "Outside of that it'll rattle your teeth, but you'll be okay."

"And inside of that?" Price asked.

"If you're within sixty feet, you'll be knocked out cold," Barnard said.

"What about thirty feet?" Price asked.

"The shock wave will probably stop your heart," Barnard said.

"They're right on our tail," the Tsar said. He sounded panicky.

"What do we do?" Wilton asked.

Chisnall raised his head above the level of the deck. It was clear. The stern was lined with equipment lockers but nothing large enough to conceal a person. On the right side of the deck was an inflatable boat, a Zodiac, on a short slipway for easy launching.

He slid onto the deck and crawled behind the Zodiac. Only then did he raise himself up and peer forward. He didn't have his night-vision mask, but he didn't need it. The deck was well lit by fluorescent tubes mounted on the superstructure above him. A large window at the top opened onto the bridge, and he could see someone moving around inside.

He eased past the Zodiac, toward an open door. Inside, he could see some of the Demon Team. Three of them were conscious but looked dazed, sitting cross-legged, leaning against a wall. Their hands were locked to their necks in a neckcuff, a type of Bzadian handcuff. Two others were lying on the floor, but their hands also were cuffed, which gave him some hope that they were still alive. One of them was bleeding from the ear. Varmint was missing.

He waited outside, listening for a guard. There had to be a guard. He couldn't wait long. At any moment someone could decide to walk back to the stern, or someone up on the bridge could look down.

At any moment the boat could reach the Angel Team.

He was unarmed. His weapons were stored in the equipment pod towed behind Monster's DPV. But there was no time, so there was no choice. He moved forward, sliding his feet across the wet deck to minimize noise. When he reached the door, he stopped again to listen and, hearing nothing, risked a quick glance inside. An internal flight of stairs led up to the bridge. There was an open door at the bottom of the stairs, and he could clearly hear the crew talking, discussing some new sonar contacts.

The Angels.

Just the sound of the Bzadian tongue sent a cold chill down his spine. Hearing it made everything much more real. He really was once again behind enemy lines, walking a very precarious tightrope. Chisnall slipped into the cabin and shut the door at the bottom of the stairs. The voices from the bridge became an indistinct murmur. Good. The door was soundproof.

He ran over to the first of the Demons and kneeled beside him. Dazed eyes stared up at him. Chisnall had never seen the effects of an ultrasound blast at close range. It wasn't pretty. Blood trickled from the Demon's nose. His name was Miscreant, Chisnall thought, although all the Demons seemed to look the same—skinny, hard-faced, and with a shaved head. Miscreant had an even scrawnier look about him, which was how Chisnall recognized him. The next two Demons, Yobbo and Hooligan, seemed equally dazed and confused.

Chisnall examined Miscreant's neckcuff. A flexible plastic collar with two wrist loops fastened at the back of the neck. Struggling or pulling on the wrist loops only tightened the collar, choking the prisoner until he or she relaxed. The locking mechanism was a simple one, requiring a key-tube to be pushed into a hole at the back of the neck. Chisnall didn't have a key-tube. He could probably get the Demons over the side of the boat, but even conscious they would drown with their hands locked to their necks.

"Stop what you are doing," a voice said, slow and even, and Chisnall looked up to see a steady coil-gun aimed right at his head. The Bzadian who held it was unusually tall and thick-chested: tough and competent.

Chisnall stood up, folding his arms across his chest, Bzadian style, with his palms out, to indicate that he was not going to resist.

"What have you done to these soldiers?" Chisnall asked. The language and the regional dialect flowed effortlessly, his surgically created forked tongue buzzing on the difficult Bzadian sounds. "We were on a training exercise in the bay and found ourselves attacked by our own forces."

"A training exercise?" the Bzadian said. "Why didn't we know about it?"

"Of course you knew about it," Chisnall said. He turned as he spoke, bending down over the scrawny shape of Miscreant and examining the blood that trickled from his ear. "The exercise has been planned for weeks. Coastal Defense Command knows all about it. Now you have killed some of my best soldiers."

There was a clear pulse in Miscreant's neck, but the Bzadian wouldn't be able to see that.

"They were all alive when we brought them on board," the Bzadian said.

"Alive? I don't think so. Not with a bullet in the back of his head!" Chisnall said.

"What?"

"See for yourself," Chisnall said, and the Bzadian came closer. "I want to speak to your captain immediately. And get Coastal Defense on the radio. Tell them . . ."

Chisnall never finished the sentence. Bending down had been an excuse to shift his weight onto the balls of his feet. He exploded upward, hitting the Bzadian's midriff, just below the coil-gun he was carrying. The gun became a club, smashing into the Bzadian's face. Anyone else would have gone down at that point, but this one seemed to be made of rock. He grunted and staggered back a few steps. He was smart too. He didn't try to bring the coil-gun to bear; it would never have worked in that confined space. He dropped the gun and swung an elbow at Chisnall's head. It exploded into his temple, rocking him sideways.

Chisnall didn't want to get into a boxing match with someone who seemed to have been carved out of granite. Instead, he put the Bzadian on the deck with a quick judo move, slipping his leg behind the Bzadian's legs and pushing him backward. The Bzadian grunted as his head hit the deck but shook it off and punched upward with both fists. Chisnall flicked his head sideways and the blow glanced his cheek. Had the blow connected solidly, the fight would have been over there and then.

Chisnall kneed him in the stomach, forcing the air from his lungs, but the Bzadian's hands were around his neck, pulling him down. With a sudden shift of his body weight, the Bzadian was on top of him and the metal cable from his coil-gun was around his neck. Chisnall could feel the metal dig into his skin. Black spots danced in front of his eyes. He tried to bring his legs up, to twist himself out of the other's grasp, but he was too firmly pinned.

The muscles of his chest started to spasm as they heaved to find air that would not come.

Price didn't need sonar to hear the churning sounds of the propellers through the water.

"Here it comes!" the Tsar yelled.

"What do we do?" Wilton asked. "What do we do?"

"Dive deep," Price said. "Get as far as you can from the bomb."

"No! Surface!" Barnard yelled.

"Which?" Monster asked.

"Surface," Barnard said. "After the depth charge hits the water, there will be a delay while it sinks. Try and get your head and as much of your body as possible out of the water before it explodes."

"Why?" Price asked.

"The air-water barrier," Barnard said. "The surface of the water acts like a mirror for sound. Ninety percent of the sonic boom will be reflected back down."

"Do it," Price said. "Tsar, let us know the second the bomb hits the water."

"You'll know it!" the Tsar said.

"As soon as you hear it, unplug your sonar," Barnard said. "If you want to have any ears left afterward."

A loud thud penetrated through the roaring in Chisnall's ears, and the pressure on his neck released. Vision returned and with it an image that Chisnall could not at first comprehend. A wet-suited figure was standing over him, a metal pipe in his hand.

"What the hell was that Puke made of?" the figure asked, its face gradually coming into focus. It was the Demon leader, Varmint. "I had to hit him twice before he went down," he said.

The Bzadian was lying unconscious beside Chisnall, blood flowing freely from a head wound.

Varmint extended a hand, helping Chisnall to his feet.

"Thanks," Chisnall said. His lips seemed to be made of clay.

"What the hell are you doing here?" Varmint asked. "I had everything under control."

"Let's get your guys out of here," Chisnall said. They could argue about it later.

Varmint had already found a key-tube on the Bzadian and was uncuffing his team. One was trying to sit up now, consciousness gradually returning.

Chisnall grabbed a couple of the neckcuffs, thinking that they might come in handy. He moved to the doorway and checked outside.

"Where are you going?" Varmint asked.

"You look after your guys," Chisnall said. "I'm going to try and save mine. See if you can launch the Zodiac without anyone noticing. I'll stay on your comm channel. When I give you the word, make some noise."

"What's your plan?" Varmint asked.

"I'll tell you when I figure that out," Chisnall said.

Most of the Demons were on their feet now, two of them helping Yobbo, who must have taken the worst of the blast. He was still unconscious but breathing steadily.

"Hey, Chisnall," Varmint said as Chisnall headed for the doorway.

He glanced back. "Yeah?"

Varmint gave him a short nod. "Thanks. For coming to help."

"You'd have done the same," Chisnall said.

"Not a fat rat's chance in hell," Varmint said, grinning.

Chisnall smiled and slipped out through the doorway, up a short flight of steps, and onto a starboard passageway that extended the length of the ship. Low deck lights cast oval pools of amber across the deck.

He padded forward. Shouting came from the bow of the ship, and a group of Bzadians was clustered around the rails. The sea was incandescent, lit by a pair of underwater search-lights. As he neared the bow, he could see the squat shape of the depth-charge launcher, a simple catapult-like device with a cradle for the depth charge, which was about the size and shape of a two-liter soda bottle, with stubby fins at the bottom. He had to get to it before it fired, or it would be the Angels floating facedown on the surface of the ocean with blood trickling from their ears and noses. But to get to it, he would have to get past at least seven or eight Bzadians, who were leaning over the railings, peering down at the gleaming water.

Even as he was trying to formulate a plan, the long arm of the launcher flicked skyward in a whiplash-like motion, catapulting the depth charge into the air. It disappeared from sight in the black of the sky, and he instinctively started counting as he waited for the explosion.

■ ■ ■

The waiting was the hardest part, Price thought. In a few seconds she would either be alive or dead, and there was little she could do to affect things either way. She looked around for Monster but couldn't see him.

"Splashdown!" the Tsar yelled, and Price twisted the throttle of her barracuda. The craft began to rise.

"Come on!" she yelled, as if that would make it go faster.

The water around her was alive with the powerful searchlights from the rapidly closing ship.

Her barracuda broke surface, like a fish jumping at an insect, just as there was a roar below and the shock wave hit. Her legs felt like they had been sledgehammered, all the way up to her waist, but her vital chest and stomach were clear of the water.

Barnard had been right, Price realized. Safety lay above the surface of the water. Her legs felt bruised but otherwise okay.

Not so for her barracuda. The ultrasonic sound wave had smashed into it, crumpling the light tailfin structure and ripping off the bow. It began to sink, grabbing at her leg and threatening to take her down with it until she kicked herself clear. Her air tube snagged on something and ripped the mask from her face, spiraling with the broken barracuda to the depths of the ocean. With the mask went her night vision, although that was hardly necessary. The lights of the ship were turning night into day.

She dived back below the surface as coil-gun projectiles *zizz*ed through the water around her. The lights of the ship grew in size as it bore down on her position, and she swam frantically, desperate to get out of its path before it ran her down.

The ship passed her by with a growl of propellers, the kick of the bow wave shunting her aside. She was weaponless. Helpless. Trapped in the open ocean.

The ship heeled over, circling around for another run.

The Bzadian crew were reloading the launcher, slotting another of the stubby ultrasonic bombs onto the cradle. The deck-mounted searchlights swiveled around to the left as the deck tilted beneath Chisnall's feet, the ship turning sharply.

"Varmint, go loud," he whispered.

Somewhere behind him and off to port, the Zodiac's engine started with a roar.

The crew shouted and pointed as they gathered on the port side of the vessel.

Chisnall raced forward, just behind the enemy soldiers, but unnoticed.

He reached for the depth charge, then stopped himself. What could he do with it? The Bzadians would simply replace it with another.

His hand brushed against something hanging from his utility belt. The neckcuffs!

He grabbed one and clipped it around the base of the depth charge, just above the fins, securing it to the cradle. Backing away, he ducked below an equipment locker as one of the Bzadians turned and glanced at the launcher.

The ship was still slanted as it circled around on a tight

loop. He had hoped they would chase the Zodiac, but instead they were turning around for another run at the Angels.

Several of the Bzadians crossed just in front of him.

He slid back and whispered into his comm, "Price, this is Chisnall. How copy?"

"Clear copy, LT. We're in the water. Most of the barracudas are out of action." Price's voice sounded calm.

"Okay, on my mark, dive down, as deep as you can," Chisnall said.

"Negative," Price said. "We have to try and get up out of the water before the next depth charge."

"Price, listen," Chisnall said. "There's no time to explain. On my mark, get under the water, stay there as long as you can. It's your only chance!"

"Solid copy," Price said.

The ship straightened as it completed its turn and began its second run. The arm of the launcher drew down.

There was a shout behind Chisnall. He spun to see two Bzadians running up the passageway. One was firing at him, but the shots were going wild on the unsteady deck of the ship.

There was a whiplash sound from the launcher and the catapult arm snapped upward.

Three seconds.

The Bzadians were either scanning the water for the splash or distracted by the shooting. None of them seemed to have realized that the depth charge was hanging from the cradle of the launcher, tethered by the neckcuff around its tailfins.

He leaped up from his hiding place and sprinted. A bullet tugged at his arm and another sparked off the side rail beside him.

"Now!" Chisnall shouted. "Get under *now*!"

Two.

The Bzadians at the bow were turning now, faces wide with shock as he burst through the middle of them, hurdling the guardrail and swan-diving toward the water.

One.

The water rushed up to meet him as the world turned to thunder.

5. ST. HELENA

[2305 hours local time]
[Bzadian Patrol Boat: QW-67, Moreton Bay, New Bzadia]

"QW-67, THIS IS COASTAL DEFENSE COMMAND. WHAT IS your status?"

The sound of the radio echoed down the stairs from the bridge above. The speaker was female, and although speaking in standard Bzadian, she had a slight accent that Chisnall couldn't identify.

"QW-67, this is Coastal Defense Command. Can you hear me?"

Chisnall ignored it and concentrated on what he was doing, which was searching the pockets of the ship's captain.

They were in the main cabin, below the bridge. The ultrasonic blast of the depth charge had smashed every window on the ship and damaged a lot of the electronic equipment. Stalled in the water and drifting with the currents, it was now a ghost ship, silent, dark, nobody conscious on board.

The Demons had hunted around in the black waters on the Zodiac and hauled each of the Angels on board before returning to the ship. Now they were working their way through the cabins, neckcuffing crew members until they ran out of cuffs and tying the rest with rope.

Monster, who said he knew a little bit about boats, was up on the bridge, trying to work out the ship's controls and restart the engines before the ship wandered too far.

Wilton and one of the Demons had taken the Zodiac to try to locate the equipment pods.

"We're wasting our time," Price said. She finished tying up one of the Bzadian crew members and rolled him over in a corner with the others. "It's after eleven. We've missed the shift change."

"Thanks to these amateurs," the Tsar said with a contemptuous glance at one of the Demons.

Varmint was giving some medical treatment to one of his team. He looked up. "You're real tough, aren't you, pretty boy? You want to come over here and say that?"

"If it wasn't for you screaming out your location, the ship would never have found us," the Tsar said.

"That's enough, Tsar," Chisnall said.

Varmint walked over and stood nose to nose with the Tsar, who didn't flinch. "Our sonar unit malfunctioned. Started active pinging all by its ownself. You got a problem with how we handled it, you talk to me."

"'All by its ownself,'" the Tsar repeated.

"Yeah, that's right, half-wit," Miscreant said, going to stand by his leader. "All by its ownself."

Price moved up alongside the Tsar. "Maybe you should have checked it before the mission," she said.

She looked wiry and mean. Of the two of them, she was the far more dangerous, Chisnall thought, and wondered if Varmint realized that.

"Maybe we did, but someone tampered with it," Varmint said.

Chisnall froze. His breath caught in his throat.

Was that possible? Could there be another traitor among the human forces? On the last mission, a traitor had nearly cost him his life.

He had taken no chances on this trip. He had personally checked all the Angel Team's barracudas, then supervised their stowing into the equipment lockers on the submarine.

But he hadn't thought to inspect the Demons' equipment.

Barnard was checking knots on a group of Bzadians at the back of the room. Chisnall caught a curious exchange of glances between her and Varmint.

"It couldn't have been tampered with," Chisnall said. "The entire navy base was declared a top-security area prior to the mission. And the wharves were sealed off."

"Except for the navy crews," Varmint said. "And your guys."

The words hung in the air, an unspoken accusation.

"And yours," Price said.

Varmint laughed, a short bark. "My guys, I trust. They've been with me a long time. How well do you know your team, Chisnall?"

Chisnall said nothing. He had to speak; he knew that. His team would be expecting him to back them up. But how well *did* he know his team? Monster, Price, and Wilton, yes. After Uluru there was no doubt. But Barnard and the Tsar were new. Did he really trust them?

"Maybe your sonar was faulty," the Tsar said into Chisnall's silence. "Did you think about that before you started hurling accusations?"

"Do me a favor and don't try to think," Varmint said. "Just concentrate on looking pretty."

"Idiot," Miscreant said.

"None of us sabotaged your equipment," Price said. "And you wouldn't be here now if we hadn't come to your rescue."

Yobbo rose and stood next to the other Demons. Hooligan joined them. Four of them faced down the two Angels. Barnard stayed where she was and Chisnall found himself still unable to move. The terrifying thought of another traitor, possibly in his own team, had made his blood freeze.

"You rescued us? I don't think so, little girl," Yobbo said. "Our skipper had everything under control, until your LT blundered in and nearly got himself killed."

"He saved your lives, little boy," Price said.

“That lily-livered wimp bag couldn’t even save himself,” Miscreant said with a meaningful glance at Chisnall, who was still crouched over the unconscious body of the ship’s captain.

“Wimp bag?” Price said, her eyes gleaming, her fists clenching and unclenching.

A sharp breath of wind lashed the ship with a high-pitched whine and the floor lurched beneath them. From the bridge came the sound of smashing glass as a broken pane fell out of its frame. One of the Bzadians groaned and stirred.

There was a gentle cough from the staircase that led up to the bridge, and Monster was there, backlit by the light from the top of the stairs.

“Monster was with Chisnall at Uluru,” he said. “If he is wimp bag, then Monster is a big girl’s handbag.” He grinned. “Is Monster a big girl’s handbag?”

“Uh-oh, it’s smiling,” Chisnall said, finally finding his voice. He stood up. “I hate it when it smiles like that. You can never tell if it wants to hug you or if it’s about to tear you limb from limb.”

The bulky shape advanced down the stairs to stand right behind Price.

“Monster, try to leave some of them alive,” Chisnall said. Monster grinned again and there was something primal about the way he bared his teeth, like a wild dog preparing to attack.

Varmint held Monster’s gaze for a moment, then snorted and turned away. “We’re out of here as soon as the Zodiac gets back,” he said.

The others followed him out of the rear door.

Price spun around to face Monster. She pushed him in the chest, thrusting him backward. "What was that all about?"

"Four on two. Was not fair fight."

"Oh, sure. Like I can't stick up for myself," Price said. "Now they think I'm weak."

"He was only trying to help," the Tsar said.

"Did I look like I needed his help?" Price said with a withering glare at the Hungarian. "Did I ask for his help?"

Price wasn't really angry with Monster for backing them up. Chisnall could sense that. She was just making noise to cover for the fact that Chisnall should have jumped in and hadn't.

Price started to say more but stopped as Wilton appeared at the rear door, dripping with water.

"Did you find the equipment pods?" Chisnall asked, grateful for the interruption.

"Yes, both," Wilton said. "Both Oscar Kilo. They're on the stern deck." He looked around. "Everything all right?"

"Just Sergeant Price and Monster having a lover's tiff," Barnard said.

"Get puked," Price said.

Varmint stuck his head back through the door. "See ya, kiddies. Try not to hurt yourselves playing with the big boys' toys."

"Get going," Chisnall said. "The task force will be at the river mouth in less than an hour."

"Only if you do your job," Varmint said.

"I think we'll cope," Chisnall said. "Get out of here."

"Have fun, boys," Price said. "Try not to blow your nuts off. Oh, too late."

A single-finger salute came back through the doorway as Varmint disappeared.

"Exactly how will we 'cope'?" Barnard asked.

"We've missed the shift change," the Tsar said. "The next one is not for four hours."

"How will we even get to the island?" Wilton asked. "Most of the barracudas are out of action or missing. Those that are still working are damaged. They'd hear us coming a mile away."

Chisnall was silent. He had no answer. They called him Lieutenant Lucky, but good luck had been in short supply so far on this mission.

He walked to the rear of the room and out onto the stern deck. The lights of the island were so close, but so far out of their reach. The wind gusted again, rocking the ship, still powerless and at the mercy of the waves.

The Demons were unhooking the Zodiac from the winch cables, and as he watched, the motor started, the bow lifted, and the Demons ducked beneath a spray of water as the boat powered away.

"Even if we get to the island, the Pukes won't be expecting another shift change." Price's voice sounded softly right behind him. "We'd have to fight our way in. There's no way."

Chisnall didn't look around but kept his eyes on the island.

"There'll be a way," he said, wishing he felt more confident that that was true.

"I don't see how—" Price said.

Chisnall cut her off, aware that his voice was rising but unable to help himself. "Neither do I, Sergeant Price, but I do see that if we can't make this happen, then the mission is cactus. The Bzadians are sitting in the White House by Valentine's Day, and by the end of the year the human race is gone the way of the dinosaurs. So no, I don't see how either, but we're going to do it anyway."

He turned and saw she was not alone. The rest of the team had emerged from the cabin and was standing alongside Price. There was an uncomfortable silence, and he realized it was the first time he had raised his voice to his team like that. The silence grew, and he wanted to fill it, to apologize, but a leader could not do that. It would seem weak.

"I have an idea," Barnard said.

"Let's hear it," Chisnall said.

"Let's go and knock on the front door," Barnard said, smiling. "They won't be expecting that."

Chisnall found himself staring at the German girl. So were the others. There was something different about her. It took him a moment to realize that it was the first time he had seen her smile. She had done it deliberately, he felt, a calculated move to defuse the tension.

"How are we even going to get to the front door?" Wilton asked.

"You're standing on it," Barnard said. "We take the ship. Tell them we're in trouble and need to put into their wharf for repairs."

"Might work." Chisnall looked at Monster. "Can you get her started?"

Monster nodded. "Think so."

"Show me," Chisnall said. "Price, you come too. You other guys find some rags and tape and gag the Pukes. The last thing we need is for them to start yelling and screaming when we get to the island."

He followed Monster to the bridge, broken glass crunching under their feet. Monster pressed a few buttons and the engine roared before settling into a quiet rumble.

"You seem to know what you're doing," Chisnall said.

Monster grinned.

"He should. His father was a ship's captain," Price said.

"In Hungary? I thought it was landlocked," Chisnall said, wondering how Price knew that and he didn't.

"There is a little river called Danube," Monster said. "Perhaps you have heard of it."

"Okay, smart-ass," Chisnall said. "Just drive the boat."

Monster grinned. He pointed to the controls. "Engines and steering fine. Deck gun seem to be working, although we won't know for sure unless we fire. Radar, she is broken, but radio is working."

Right on cue, the radio crackled back to life.

"QW-67, this is Coastal Defense Command. What is your status?"

Chisnall ignored it and lowered the volume. He turned his comm off and stared at the other two.

Price went off comm also. "Feel the need to talk, LT?" she asked.

Monster switched his comm off as well.

"You hear what Varmint said?" Chisnall asked.

"About the barracudas?" Monster asked. "You think could be true? We have traitor?"

"You guys and Wilton, I trust," Chisnall said. "Barnard and the Tsar . . ."

"Barnard scares the doo-doo out of me," Monster said.

Chisnall almost laughed at the idea of anything scaring the doo-doo out of Monster but stopped himself. He knew exactly what Monster meant.

"She's not the one you should be afraid of," Price said.

"What do you mean?"

"I don't like her either," Price said. "But when the brown stuff hits the fan, I'd trust her to watch my back."

"But not the Tsar?" Chisnall asked.

"The Hero of Hokkaido?" Price snorted. "Not so much."

"Any reason?" Chisnall asked.

"Not really. He's loud and obnoxious, and I bet he never met a mirror he didn't like, but I'm just not sure that what we're seeing is what we're getting."

"That's no basis to call him a traitor," Chisnall said. "And he has as much reason as any of us to hate the Pukes."

"Are you sure about that?" Price said.

"His family are Bzadian slaves," Chisnall said.

"Or maybe they're bargaining chips," Price said.

"Bargaining chips?" Chisnall asked.

"If the Pukes have somehow identified the Tsar as a member of Angel Team, they could be holding his family hostage."

"Angel Team is top secret," Monster said. "Pukes don't know who we are or who our families are."

"Who knows how much they really know," Price said. "Who knows if there are other moles like Brogan."

It took a great effort for Chisnall not to wince at the mention of her name.

"Maybe Demon sonar really was just faulty," Monster said.

"Yeah, and maybe that ship just happened to be in the bay tonight," Price said. "Or maybe someone doesn't want the mission to succeed."

"Okay, so the Tsar is a suspect," Chisnall said. "But I'm not sure Barnard is quite who she says she is either. There's not enough evidence to convict either of them, so from now on keep a close eye on them both."

He stopped for a moment, thinking, then said, "Send Barnard up. I want to hear more about this idea of hers."

"Coastal Defense Command, this is QW-67," Chisnall said in Bzadian, and released the mike switch.

The island was a large mass ahead of them. Monster was driving the ship and seemed to be doing a good job.

The radio was answered after a few seconds.

"QW-67, what is your status?" It was the same female voice as before.

"An accident with the thunderclap launcher," Chisnall said. "One of the charges jammed on the cradle and exploded on the deck."

"We heard that from here. Thought the whole ship had exploded. Casualties?"

"A few burst eardrums and concussions, nothing more. It knocked out a bit of equipment, though. It's taken us this long to get systems back up and running." Chisnall paused, then said, "We have only just got the radio working."

"QW-67, who is speaking?"

"First Officer Gkuzhin," Chisnall replied. He had taken the name from the ID of one of the Bzadian crew.

"Where is Captain u'Zout?"

"He was injured in the blast," Chisnall replied. "He is being attended to by the medical officer."

There was a brief silence on the radio, then: "Please proceed immediately to the port at Brisbane."

"Negative. We are heading for St. Helena Island. It's pitch-black out here. We have no working lights or navigation systems, and they have the nearest wharf. We will assess damage there and proceed to the port at first light."

"Affirmative, QW-67. We will advise the SONRAD station that you're coming."

"Knock-knock," Chisnall murmured without keying the radio. That earned a brief smile from Barnard.

"What is the status of the soldiers you picked up from the water?" Coastal Command asked.

"They are down in the main cabin," Chisnall said, guessing where this was going. "They are secured."

"We have checked with all operational units in the area, and none are conducting a training exercise tonight."

Chisnall held his breath, trying to work out what to say next.

Barnard said, "Ask her what she thinks."

Chisnall nodded. That was a smart move. "What is your assessment of the situation, Coastal Command?" he asked.

"We are still working on that," came the reply.

"Now plant the idea that they could be Fezerker," Barnard said.

Chisnall looked at her. Evaluating her. They had told him she was smart. They just hadn't told him *how* smart. That in itself was a worry. She was certainly smart enough to fool him. As Brogan had been.

To Coastal Command, he said, "One of my crew thinks they may be Fezerker." The Fezerker units, almost a Bzadian equivalent of Recon Team Angel, were so ultrasecret that their existence had not been confirmed until Uluru. That had worked to the Angels' advantage then, and it might again now. The Fezerkers' operations were so clandestine that not even the Coastal Defense Command would know their movements.

He got the reaction he wanted from Coastal Command.

"Fezerker." The voice sounded hushed, as if she did not want to be heard.

"Can you find out anything?" Chisnall asked.

"I will try," she said. "The SONRAD station picked up your Zodiac a while ago, heading into port."

"Spare parts," Barnard murmured.

"They have gone to find some spare parts for our repairs," Chisnall said.

"Understood," the voice said.

Chisnall hung the microphone back on the hook by the steering controls. "You think they fell for it?" he asked.

"We'll know when we get to the island," Barnard said.

"How's she handling, Monster?" Chisnall asked.

"The ship, she is doing fine," Monster said.

"Do you think you'll be able to dock her cleanly at the wharf?" Chisnall asked. "It will make the Pukes a bit suspicious if we ram the boat into the wharf when we try to dock."

"Monster will do his best," he said.

Chisnall nodded. No matter what the situation, Monster's *best* would always be good enough.

He turned his attention to the large video screens that were mounted on the ceiling, showing the view from outside in every direction. He focused on the weapons station. The ship's only gun was an M242 Bushmaster, a twenty-five-millimeter chain-fed autocannon mounted on the front deck.

He sat down and examined the unit. A series of cables ran into the top of a metal console. In the center was a screen that showed a view from the gun barrel. A thin cross indicated the aiming point. Buttons and lights to the left of the screen indicated the status of the Rafael Typhoon gun mount, while similar buttons to the right of the screen showed the status of the weapon itself. The firing controls appeared to be triggers on twin joysticks below the screen.

After a short time playing around with the controls, he was able to preselect targets and lock them in. The automatic fire control would register the visual signature of each target and automatically acquire them again at the press of a button.

The gun was on the bow of the vessel, in front of the superstructure, and was very close to the depth-charge launcher where the blast had happened. Chisnall was surprised that it had come through unscathed but was happy that it seemed to be working. Just in case.

"Where on the island is the wharf?" he asked.

"To west, at the end of spit," Monster said, glancing at a chart laid out in the center of the bridge.

"Head to the east side. We'll circle around the island counterclockwise," Chisnall said.

"What you are thinking?" Monster asked.

"I'm going to be prepared," Chisnall said. "I'm going to send in the Phantom."

Monster grinned. "God help the Bzadians."

6. KRIZ

[2325 hours local time]
[Bzadian Coastal Defense Command, Brisbane, New Bzadia]

MAJOR ZARA KRIZ WAS NERVOUS, ALTHOUGH THERE was no clear reason to be. She stroked the soft new skin of her forearm and stared at the notes she had written on the electronic log in front of her.

She was the ranking duty officer, responsible for a staff of four junior officers, all of whom had been on the job much longer than she had.

She had been there for two months, assigned to the command center while she was recovering in the hospital, but most of that time she had been learning, training. Only in the last week had she been entrusted with the duty officer role.

She stroked her forearm again. She did that when she was nervous, running her fingers across the scar where the newly grown baby skin of her forearm met the older, coarser skin of her upper arm.

The patrol ship, QW-67, had been investigating a strange pinging reported by the SONRAD station on St. Helena Island. The commander of the ship had taken it upon himself to depth-charge the contact, but a depth charge had malfunctioned, damaging equipment and injuring the ship's crew. Worse, the contact appeared to be a military unit—Bzadian, not human—probably on some kind of exercise. That made it a "friendly fire" incident, which meant a full investigation.

Was that the reason for her nervousness? Or was it the possibility that there was more to this than met the eye?

She had been at Uluru when the audacious scumbugz attack had taken place, right in the heart of New Bzadia.

A firestorm of missiles had pounded the biggest Bzadian military base on the planet. She had been in a rotorcraft with the rest of her squad. They had just taken off when they were hit.

She was the only survivor.

Doctors had rebuilt her shattered body and regrown her burned skin, but after that day nothing on this planet—or any other—could persuade her to get back onto a rotorcraft. They had to sedate her to transport her between hospitals.

A soldier who's afraid to fly was of no use to the military, so she was now stuck behind a desk.

But she remembered Uluru. If humans had once been prepared to launch an attack inside New Bzadia, they might be prepared to do so again.

Of course, there was no evidence of that. Was there? Merely a training exercise gone wrong and a malfunctioning bomb.

So why was her hand endlessly rubbing the new skin?

Better to err on the side of caution, she decided.

She tapped her video screen to bring it to life and punched in a code.

A face appeared on the screen almost immediately. A young man in the uniform of a plant operator.

“SONRAD communications,” he said. “I am Hez.”

7. THE LONGEST NIGHT

[2335 hours local time]
[St. Helena Island, Moreton Bay, New Bzadia]

PRICE SLITHERED FORWARD IN THE LIGHTLY BREAKING waves on the east side of the island, her eyeline just above water. She bobbed her head up and down with the waves, ducking down in the troughs to minimize her profile in case there were any watchers.

As far as she could tell, there were none.

She eased herself out of the water, almost invisible in her black wet suit, and snaked across the beach. The dark, muddy sand quickly healed itself, erasing the marks of her passage. Above her, on the highest points of the island, one to the north and one to the south, luminous geodesic spheres, like massive soccer balls, hid the spinning radar antennas.

She liked the taste of the salt water on her lips, the feel of the mud between her fingers. Here, she was in her element. On her own, operating in shards of darkness where no one would think to look. Dependent on no one. Responsible for no one. From her youngest days this had been her best defense and her most powerful weapon. If you didn't get noticed, you didn't get hurt.

To the north, the lights of the ship were heading toward the point. She checked the time. Less than fifteen minutes.

Price crawled forward and pulled up the waterproof equipment bag she had attached by a cord to her ankle. It contained a Bzadian security guard's uniform, night-vision goggles, a pistol, and a can of Puke spray.

The beach gave way to a sticky mangrove swamp that provided good cover, although the mud sucked at her arms and legs as she crawled through it in the blackness. Clouds of insects rose around her. The thought of snakes crossed her mind, but she pushed the image away. She wouldn't see one until she crawled on top of it, even with the aid of the NV goggles.

Thirteen minutes.

Chisnall checked the time on his wrist computer. It was going to be tight. They were taking the long way around to give Price as much time as possible, but she still had to slip onto the island, get inside the complex, and take out the power before the ship got to the wharf. If anyone could do it, it was the Phantom, but there was so little time.

The equipment pod lay open on the deck, and the team was helping themselves to weapons and ammunition. They were dressed in the uniforms of the Bzadian ship's crew. That crew—some conscious, some naked, all resentful—were secured inside and out of sight.

Wilton snorted as he took an ammunition pack for his coil-gun. "We might as well throw rocks at them," he said.

The others grunted in agreement.

The success of the first Angel mission at Uluru had not been kept quiet for long. Nor had the second, a rescue mission on the island of Hokkaido in Japan.

Rumors had started spreading through the military, and within weeks it was common knowledge in the Free Territories that teams of teenage soldiers were engaged in missions behind enemy lines. What the human public didn't know was the extent to which the Angels and Demons had gone to disguise themselves as Bzadians. Nor the extensive training they had received in Bzadian languages and customs.

But the knowledge of the Angel Team caused an uproar in the free media. *Child Soldiers!* roared one conservative newspaper. *Babes in Arms!* declared another.

The outcry from left-wing groups had been so great that ACOG had been forced to issue only nonlethal weapons to the Angel and Demon teams.

"The human race is on the verge of extinction and they won't let us fight with real guns?" Wilton said.

"Clearly it is better to be dead than risk being politically incorrect," Barnard said.

"I agree, but we're going to have to live with it," Chisnall said.

Their coil-guns were real, but their ammunition was not. Instead of metal-jacketed bullets, the Angels had "puffer" pellets. Made of a compacted powder, they disintegrated on impact with body armor, instantly vaporizing into a cloud of particles. The thump of the bullet on chest armor was powerful enough to knock the wind out of the target's lungs. As they gasped air back in, they breathed in the particles. They were unconscious before they realized they'd been shot.

The Angels' sidearms also were loaded with puffers. They were M9 pistols, human weapons, because the Bzadian needle-guns could not take a puffer pellet.

Both types of weapon were silenced. The M9s had a long dimpled tube screwed onto the end of the barrel, while the coil-guns had lowered the speed of the projectiles so they didn't break the sound barrier on the way out of the barrel. They could be dialed back up later if need be, but for this part of the mission, stealth and silence were all-important.

The only other weapon the Angels were officially allowed (other than smoke and stun grenades) was K-122 spray. A simple aerosol spray in a pressurized can, it contained a chemical that had little effect on humans but caused a crippling paralysis to Bzadians. It lasted for hours, leaving them conscious but unable to move a muscle. It smelled of peppermint and had been nicknamed *Puke spray*.

Wilton loaded a clip of puffer bullets into his coil-gun and checked the action, sliding it back and forth a few times.

It was more of a habit than a necessity. Bzadian guns never jammed.

"I heard one of the Demons say they were going to exchange the puffers for real ammunition as soon as they hit dry land," he said.

"They can do what they like. We're not," Chisnall said.

"Puffers aren't that bad," Barnard said. "You can hit Bzadian body armor two or three times with metal bullets and they still keep on shooting at you. Hit them once in the right spot with a puffer, and they're down. Not permanently, but long enough."

"Yeah, but you gotta hit them in exactly the right spot," Wilton said.

"Since when has this been a problem for you?" Barnard asked.

"Since, I dunno, never," Wilton admitted.

Chisnall smiled. Wilton's reputation as a sharpshooter was widespread. It was said that he could shoot the eye out of a fast-moving eagle at five hundred meters and then shoot out the other eye.

"In any case, orders are orders," Chisnall said.

About a hundred feet into the mangrove swamp, Price hit firm ground—a track that led into the heart of the island.

After a quick debate with herself, she decided to take it. There might be alarms or booby traps along the track, but her progress through the swamp was so slow that she wasn't going to make it to the complex before the ship reached the wharf if she didn't find a faster way. The track was dead straight and seemed clear. It headed due east, toward the northernmost of the two geodesic radar spheres.

A six-foot-high razor-wire fence marked the point where the swamp met solid ground. It was marked with Bzadian high-voltage symbols. Behind the fence was a line of trees. The ground was damp from the previous day's rain, and one of the fence posts was fizzing and sparking as the water reacted with the surging electric current.

With time slipping away, Price skirted along the fence until she found a branch that grew out over the fence. She tossed her equipment bag up and over the branch, keeping a hold on its long cord and catching it lightly on the other side. She twisted the two ends of the cord together, then hauled herself up until she could stretch out and lock her fingers on to the branch. A few seconds later, she was shimmying down the trunk of the tree, on the other side of the fence. She was right below the radar dome and could hear the swishing of the antenna inside the brightly lit sphere on top of the hill. She moved up to it, a short, easy climb, staying in the tree line lest the glow from the sphere reveal her to any observers.

From the peak of the hill she could see the lights of the ship, already halfway to the wharf on the western side of the island.

"I'm inside the perimeter," she murmured on her comm.

"Quick . . . can," Chisnall said. "We've . . . and rounded the . . . approaching . . ."

The comm cut in and out, and Price realized the powerful radar antenna above her was interfering with the signal from the low-powered comm radio.

"I can go faster," she said. "But not if you don't want me to be seen."

"Don't . . . seen," Chisnall said.

It was 23:43. She had less than seven minutes. She made her way through an olive grove, the branches leafy and full of fruit at this time of year. Old stone buildings rose out of the ground in front of her, roofless and crumbled, the ruins of a prison. Price moved like a ghost, flitting from shadow to shadow, with slow movements that would not catch the eye.

Below, in a small dip in the center of the island, she could see the complex of buildings that was the SONRAD station. They had all studied the satellite images. It was a modular Bzadian design. A cluster of domes, connected by plastic tubes in a shape that ACOG had nicknamed the "turtle." The turtle's body—the largest dome—was in the center and probably housed the administration offices, according to the satellite analysis experts. The turtle's legs—the four smaller domes—were supplies storage, power plant, equipment, and a vehicle garage. The turtle's head housed the sonar equipment and operators. The entrance to the complex was via the tail, a small security pod to the south.

The island's personnel was a mixture of security staff, operators who manned the radar and sonar scopes, and technicians who kept the place running smoothly.

Price cut silently through the decayed prison toward the lights of the shiny round alien buildings beyond, staying in shadows, moving to a slow beat.

The first sign she had of the security patrol was a light swaying through the olive grove behind her, flickering on the stones. She froze, pressing herself into a corner of a crumbled cell block. Phantom soldiers appeared through the olive grove, invisible behind their flashlights. Price made no movement, praying they would skirt around the old prison.

Her prayers were not answered.

Chisnall looked over at the island. Success or failure at this stage of the operation depended on his Angel Team. And his leadership. If the mission failed, it would be on his head. It wasn't a matter of pride or ego. It was the future of the human race that rode on his shoulders.

When he'd returned from Uluru, they had called him a hero.

He hadn't felt like one.

They said he had discovered, and then destroyed, the secret of Uluru.

But all he could see were the faces of the young mothers he had killed. The breeding "machines" producing crops of babies to grow up to be Bzadian spies. That they were just shells, brain-dead "vegetables," made it worse somehow, not better. They were innocents, like newborn children, not knowing or understanding the fate Chisnall had condemned them to.

"Price, hurry the hell up," he murmured, but only to himself.

Price held her breath as the security patrol passed in front of her. Two of them. The first a female, equipped with night-vision goggles, a coil-gun holstered on her back. Another soldier followed, a male.

The guards seemed alert, but not *on* alert. A routine patrol.

Price slipped the can of Puke spray out of her belt. As they passed, she followed them, using their sounds to disguise her own.

They passed the corner of a large building. The second patrol member turned, perhaps hearing a tiny sound or just somehow sensing a presence behind him. Price saw the movement in his neck and ducked back around the corner, behind a pile of stones, sinking into a pool of darkness.

The soldier paused, waiting, listening. He took a step toward Price and played his flashlight around the broken stone blocks. Another step. Now he was right alongside Price, but his light was aimed at a few bushes by the chimney behind them.

Just when Price thought he was going to move on, the beam dropped right in her eyes. The soldier jumped, startled, and opened his mouth to shout. He never got the chance. The air he inhaled was loaded with Puke spray and his tongue and vocal cords froze. His hand was reaching for his coil-gun but got only halfway there before he slumped on legs that were no longer his own.

Price caught him and lowered him to the ground. It would have been completely silent had his coil-gun not clattered on a fragment of broken stone.

"Quazig?" A voice sounded from around the corner of the building.

Price vaulted over the low wall of the ruin, into the old building, and out through the remains of a window on the other side, emerging behind the second guard as she returned to look for her colleague.

"Quazig?" Dust and small insects made vivid bright spots in the air as the soldier's flashlight rounded the corner, illuminating her comrade, motionless on the ground. Her gun jumped over her shoulder into her arms. She rushed over and kneeled beside him, checking his vital signs.

Price sensed her confusion. There were no physical marks on the soldier, and he was clearly conscious, but unmoving. She slipped behind the female soldier, as still and silent as the night. She blew softly onto the soldier's ear. The Bzadian shook her head and brushed at her ear as if annoyed by an insect.

The male's eyes flicked to Price's face, then back to his comrade's. His mouth quivered as he tried to warn her.

Price blew again, a little harder, and the Bzadian turned her head. Her eyes opened in shock and Price caught her as she dropped with a face full of spray.

With a quick glance around, Price dragged the motionless figures into the interior of the old stone ruin.

She hovered for a moment over the female soldier. Her eyes remained open, and she was breathing steadily. Her mouth moved a little—her forked tongue extending and quivering as if she wanted to say something—but she made no sound.

Price took her own Bzadian uniform out of her pack. She stripped off her wet suit, standing naked over the paralyzed guards, and reflected that if anyone came out of the buildings at that moment, it would seem a very odd scene. The guards glared at her but could do nothing else as Price quickly dressed. Her face was streaked with mud, and she wiped it off as best as she could.

Price walked casually toward the complex of buildings, as if she had every right to be there. She skirted around the first dome—the head of the turtle—then past the two smaller domes on the left side of the facility, to the tail, the entranceway to the complex. Through the open main doorway, she could see a security desk. Two guards sat there while another stood by the door.

Price frowned. Her target was the plant room, the left front leg of the turtle-shaped complex. But to get there she would have to get through the security pod. That wasn't going to be easy.

Out on the water, the lights of the ship were approaching the wharf.

A circular door slid open in the smaller dome to her right and a Land Rover roared out, followed by another, both with top-mounted fifty-caliber machine guns. Price slipped through a line of trees and saw them emerge onto a road that led down the hill, heading for the wharf.

"Angel Two to Angel One," she hissed urgently, but got only static for a reply.

"Angel Two to Angel One," she repeated. "Heavy Bzadian presence heading your way. How copy?"

Chisnall's voice came back in bite-sized chunks.

"No copy . . . Pr . . . peat."

As she watched, the vehicles reached the end of the spit and proceeded out along the wharf.

"LT, something has spooked the Pukes," she said. "Be prepared for a hostile reception!"

There was no reply but static, and she glanced up in frustration at the geodesic sphere above her. Through the trees she saw the semicircular door to the vehicle dome begin to close.

She swore under her breath and began to run toward the dome. There was nothing more she could do, except get on with her own job. Whatever happened at the wharf was up to Chisnall.

She reached the door with seconds to spare, dropped to the ground, and rolled underneath, her silenced pistol ready in her hand as the door slammed shut behind her.

A Bzadian standing behind a control desk glanced at her in confusion.

"What did you shut the door for?" Price asked.

"But . . ."

"And what are you still doing here?" Price asked, taking a few steps closer to the guard. "You're supposed to be at the front entrance."

"No, my orders are to . . ." He stopped, seeming to sense that something, somehow, was very wrong. He reached for a button on the wall.

A puff of smoke exploded from his chest and his voice gagged in his throat. He slumped forward onto the desk and then slid unconscious to the floor.

Price holstered her pistol and trotted through the vehicle garage. The open garage door had been a stroke of luck. She opened the door to the large tube that led to the central building. It was lit by long strips of fluorescent lights. A door at the far end led into the main dome. She stepped inside.

"Looks like we've got company," the Tsar said. He was on the small deck at the rear of the bridge, watching the island through binoculars. "Two vehicles approaching the wharf."

The wharf was a long strip that ran out from the end of the island. It was a basic wooden construction, empty except for a speedboat about halfway along—the boat that brought the change of shift to the island. That meant both the previous security detail and the new shift were still on the island. But Chisnall could not wait for them to leave. There simply was no time. He switched his attention to the vehicles, two Land Rovers that were hurrying down the winding road from the top of the island.

"We're not going to take any chances," he said. "What's your status, Wilton?"

"Angel Four in position," Wilton reported in. He was lying

on the roof of the bridge, in a shadow by the radar mast. His coil-gun might have been loaded with only puffers, but at that range Wilton would be able to put one on the breastbone of any enemy soldier he wanted.

"Tsar, Barnard, keep your weapons out of sight but within easy reach," Chisnall said. "I'll play captain and talk to the Pukes when we dock."

"I'll talk to them," the Tsar said. "I kind of have a knack for this stuff. Then if it starts getting hairy, I can say I have to check with my captain."

Chisnall hesitated. He wasn't sure he trusted the Tsar. But he also didn't want the Tsar to know that.

"Are you sure?" he asked.

"Too easy," the Tsar said. "I once . . ."

He launched into a story about a past mission. A perilous trek through the Chukchi Peninsula, evaluating the military buildup there, right under the noses of the Bzadians. Chisnall smiled in all the right places, but he wasn't really listening. He was watching the Tsar. Evaluating *him.*

He seems confident—too *confident,* Chisnall thought.

Monster noticed it, too, and caught Chisnall's eye. Not for the first time, Chisnall wondered about Hokkaido. The details of the mission were sealed. But they were about to find out what the Tsar was really like when bullets started flying.

"Okay, do it," Chisnall said.

Barnard stood on the rear deck, pretending to inspect some equipment. She seemed calm and collected. If one of them was a traitor, they would have to show their stripes soon.

Chisnall went inside and sat at the controls of the Bushmaster. He used a joystick to position a target indicator on the first Land Rover and locked it in as "Target A." The second Land Rover became "Target B." The weapon station would hold those targets even if they moved.

Monster, true to his word, brought the ship close up alongside the jetty. He ran the engines in reverse until the ship came to a complete halt a few yards away.

"A little closer might be better," Chisnall murmured.

"Not finished yet," Monster said, and pressed a few buttons on the controls.

A mild humming sound came from somewhere belowdecks and the ship began to drift closer to the wharf.

Chisnall raised an eyebrow.

"Magnetic mooring," Monster said. The ship came to a halt with a small thud that vibrated through the deck.

"Smooth as baby's bottom," Monster said with a grin.

Chisnall nodded. "Okay, what happens when you want to leave?"

"Reverse polarity of magnetic field, and it push you away," Monster said. He seemed to hesitate for a moment, then asked, "How is Price doing?"

"I'll find out," Chisnall murmured, and keyed his comm. "Price, how are you doing?" There was no answer. He tried again. "Price?" Still nothing. He said, "Tsar, delay them as long as you can."

The Tsar, wearing the first mate's uniform, was still out on the small top deck, his coil-gun concealed beneath a canvas tarpaulin by his feet.

Ten soldiers were standing on the wharf, while two more manned the heavy machine guns on the Land Rovers. Along with the drivers, that made fourteen. There were sixteen more guards somewhere on the island.

The Tsar saluted the waiting soldiers in the Bzadian way, with a clenched fist to his shoulder. He flashed his award-winning smile. "Thank you for allowing us to land."

He seemed relaxed but not too much. Just about right for the first mate of a boat that had been through an accidental explosion and was putting in for emergency repairs. His accent was perfect, and he leaned on the side rail like someone who had been around ships all his life.

A sergeant stepped forward and returned the salute. "We heard about the explosion. Everybody okay?"

"Apart from a few concussions and ruptured eardrums, all is good," the Tsar replied. "We were lucky."

"Do you require medical assistance?"

"Thank you, but no—our medics have everything under control."

"Our own medics are here and waiting to assist," the sergeant said.

"A kind offer, but not necessary, thanks," the Tsar said, with just the right mixture of charm and condescension. *A natural actor,* Chisnall thought. Completely convincing. That worried him a little.

"Then you will permit me to come on board and have a look around," the sergeant said.

There was a silence.

"For what reason, Sergeant? We are simply resting here till first light, while we try and repair some of our equipment," the Tsar said.

"This is a secure area," the sergeant said. "We cannot allow you to land here without a security inspection."

"Delay him," Chisnall whispered on the comm, thinking of the twenty or so Bzadian crew members tied up belowdecks. "Everyone be on your toes. When the brown stuff hits the fan, it's going to fly everywhere."

They had to wait for Price. When she took out the power, it would cut communications to the island. They couldn't take a chance that someone on the island would alert the Coastal Defense Command.

On the deck, the Tsar straightened his back and glared down at the sergeant on the wharf below. "Sergeant, this is a secure ship. We cannot allow you on board without explicit authority. We have highly sensitive information and equipment."

"I am afraid I must insist, sir," the sergeant said, making the Bzadian gesture of apology, covering his face with both hands. "Please lower your gangway and allow us to board."

"On whose authority, Sergeant?" the Tsar asked.

"On the authority of Coastal Defense Command."

"This is going to go south real fast," Chisnall murmured into the comm.

"I will have to check with my captain," the Tsar said. He turned and walked, as slowly as he could without seeming suspicious, to the door that led into the bridge. He opened it and stuck his head inside, winking at Chisnall.

Chisnall followed him out onto the deck.

"What is the problem?" he asked.

"The sergeant would like to inspect us," the Tsar said, nodding down at the wharf.

Chisnall gripped the handrail with both hands and leaned down. "Good evening, Sergeant."

"Good evening, sir," the sergeant said.

"Please repeat that, a little louder if you will," Chisnall said, tapping an ear with a finger. "I cannot hear too well. Ruptured eardrums."

"I said good evening, sir," the sergeant said loudly.

Chisnall nodded. "Please explain your request."

"We wish to board and inspect your vessel, sir."

"Would you mind repeating that slowly?" Chisnall said.

"We request to board and inspect your vessel. Sir."

"Yes, we will be inspecting the vessel for damage at first light," Chisnall said.

"You misheard me, sir," the sergeant said. "We wish to inspect your vessel."

"You wish to inspect it for us?" Chisnall asked. "Why? Are you naval engineers?"

Next to him, the Tsar had to stifle a smile.

The sergeant wasn't smiling. "Coastal Defense Command has requested a security inspection of this ship."

"A what inspection?" Chisnall said, aware that he was pushing the difficulty-hearing thing a bit too far.

"A security inspection."

"Security? Not really necessary, I can assure you, but of course, if those are your orders, we would be happy to oblige."

"Thank you, sir," the sergeant said, looking relieved.

Chisnall turned to the Tsar.

"Please organize the gangway for these soldiers."

"I'm afraid it's out of action, sir," the Tsar said.

Chisnall feigned surprise. "Well, get it working."

"That won't be necessary, sir," the sergeant said. "We have a ladder."

How convenient! Chisnall thought.

"I can have the gangway working in a couple of minutes," the Tsar said.

"Thank you, but we will board now, under direct orders from the Coastal Defense Command," the sergeant said.

"Could you please repeat that?" Chisnall said, floundering for any further way to delay them. The lights on the hill remained resolutely on. Had Price been captured or killed? He had sent her in there alone. Had he sent her to her death?

"No, sir, I can't," the sergeant said. "Please instruct your crew not to interfere with our inspection."

A short folding plastic ladder was brought out from the rear of one of the Land Rovers, unfolded, and placed against the side of the ship.

Chisnall said, "Of course, Sergeant, and welcome aboard."

Under his breath on the comm he said, "Monster, the magnetic mooring."

"Way ahead of you," Monster said.

Two soldiers moved to the ladder. One steadied it while the other began to climb. On the wharf the remainder of the soldiers watched the proceedings. Their weapons were holstered on their backs, but only a click away.

The first soldier arrived at the top of the ladder and reached out for the deck railing.

"Now," Chisnall said quietly.

There was a loud humming from below him as the magnetic polarity of the mooring device reversed. The ship eased away from the wharf. The ladder slipped, twisted, then toppled into the sea. The soldier managed to get a hand to the railing but lost his grip and fell, arms flailing into the water.

On the wharf the coil-guns of the other soldiers were now in their hands, and most of the barrels seemed to be aimed at Chisnall.

"It was an accident," Chisnall shouted. "An accident!"

Price strode to the next leg of the turtle, the power plant. An outer passageway ringed the dome, and a series of doors led to rooms in the interior. Some were open, others closed. A few eyes glanced up at her incuriously from within some of the rooms.

She grinned a little inwardly. Here she was, right in the

heart of the enemy, on her own, without backup or support. Yet here she felt the most at home. Relying on no one but herself. Wandering amid the enemy as if she owned the place.

A door appeared on the outer wall of the dome. It opened into another of the plastic walk-tubes.

She closed the door behind her and locked it, sprinting down the short circular corridor to the next door. It slid open with a sound like a loud, deep breath.

A flashing blue light filled the corridor and a siren began to wail. It was so loud that it was painful. It seared her ears and filled her head. Even the air she breathed seemed heavy, full of the sound. Price felt a moment of panic but forced it from her mind and pushed the door shut.

The power plant master switch was clearly marked, as were the controls for the backup power supply. She pressed them both and the siren and the flashing blue light cut off as the complex plunged into darkness.

"Hit them!" Chisnall yelled as the glowing radar antennae on the island blinked into darkness. The lights on the wharf also shut off, and Monster cut the ship's lights a fraction of a second later.

Chisnall had dived for the door to the bridge. The troops on the wharf, well trained and edgy, had reacted instantly. Bullets crackled through the air where he had been standing.

On the roof, Wilton's coil-gun boomed, then boomed

again. There was no need for quiet, and he had cranked the speed dial back up to full, for distance and accuracy.

The Tsar and Barnard were spraying puffer rounds at the soldiers below.

The Angels had been prepared for the sudden loss of light. The Bzadians had not. But it didn't take them long to switch to NV, and then came the staccato thunder of the machine guns from the Land Rovers.

"Get down!" Chisnall yelled, and threw himself to the floor as a series of fist-sized holes stitched a line through the wall by his head. The thin metal plating on the bridge was no match for the fifty-caliber bullets.

On the video screens he saw Barnard and the Tsar lying prone, covering their heads with their hands as the heavy machine gun chewed up the decks around them. A row of bullets splintered the deck right in front of the Tsar's face and he panicked. The Hero of Hokkaido started to get up, right in the line of fire of the fifty-cal. Chisnall knew he was dead. But Barnard's hand reached up and grabbed him by the chinstrap of his helmet, thudding his face back down onto the deck. Alive, for the moment—but not for long, the way the fifty-cal was chewing up the side of the ship.

Chisnall jumped up, ignoring the bullets, and slid into the seat of the weapon station. He punched the button for Target A and squeezed the triggers on the Bushmaster controls in one fluid movement. In an eruption of flame and smoke, one of the Land Rovers leaped up into the air, then out over the far edge of the wharf, the gunner cartwheeling off into the water. Overhead, Wilton's rifle boomed again and Chisnall saw the Bzadian sergeant drop with a surprised look on his face. He switched to Target B. The Land Rover was racing forward, trying to get to the stern of the ship, out of the big gun's zone of fire. It was shooting as it went. Bullets were ripping the wall to shreds all around Chisnall. On the screen in front of him, the electronic target indicator settled on the Land Rover and stayed there, a pipping sound indicating that the target was locked in. He squeezed the trigger just as the weapons console exploded around him, disintegrating as he ducked and tried to shield his face with his arms, metal and glass flying past him. Something smashed into his head.

The lights went out.

Price's gun was steady. The door at the far end of the corridor burst open and a burly Bzadian soldier burst through it, a flashlight glaring from the barrel of his coil-gun.

The flashlight and the weapon were aimed high and he never had a chance. Lying on the floor, her pistol aimed through a crack in the inner door, Price shot him once in the chest, lining up the next soldier even as the first collapsed, unconscious, in a cloud of puffer smoke. The second soldier, a gaunt female, stopped in her tracks as the round exploded on her armor. She stood motionless for a second; then her eyes rolled back in her head and she fell backward into the arms of the soldier behind her.

■ ■ ■

Monster was standing over Chisnall, helping him to his feet, and although he was speaking, Chisnall could not hear the words. His face felt numb and when he looked down, he saw the ruins of the weapons station lying on the floor around him. The fifty-caliber rounds must have hit just as he fired the Bushmaster.

He raced out to the deck and saw the wreckage of the second Land Rover upside down, burning on the edge of the wharf.

"We've got to get to Price," Chisnall said, his voice falling thickly on his own ears.

Weapons appeared around the edge of the door, the thunder of the coil-guns vibrating the air in the corridor. Price rolled to the left as a line of bullets cut holes in the floor where she had been lying. A grenade would have sorted things out quickly, she reflected, but would have also damaged the plant equipment. The stutter of the weapons was continuous now and impossibly loud, echoing off the smooth round surfaces of the corridor as the Bzadian troops advanced behind a shield of bullets.

She kicked the door shut. There was no way out. In just a few seconds they would burst through that door, and she would only have a puffer pistol and a can of Puke spray against a horde of deadly coil-guns.

Price rolled up onto her feet and leaped, catlike, onto the

control panel for the backup power supply. Stretching out, she sprang across to the main power plant, a huge machine in the center of the room. Her toes scrabbled for a hold on a narrow grille on the side of the machine as she tried to pull herself over the edge. Something on her belt was jammed on the top lip of the machine, but after a moment it came loose and fell to the floor with a metallic clatter. The can of Puke spray. It rolled over to the wall and came to a halt by the door. That left her with just the pistol.

She flattened herself on top of the machine as the door smashed open.

The plastic ceiling of the dome reflected the flashlights of a crowd of Bzadians bursting in, guns aimed in all directions. It would only take them a few seconds to realize that she wasn't on the floor, and only a few seconds more to work out where she must be.

Price slid forward, hoping to escape through the door. No luck. Two soldiers stood blocking the exit. The others had spread out inside the dome.

One of the soldiers by the door noticed the spray can wedged against the wall, and without lowering his weapon, reached down and picked it up.

Take a sniff, you dirty Puke, Price thought. She considered shooting the can, but she knew that the compressed powder of the puffer bullets would not be strong enough to penetrate the metal skin.

Behind her, a soldier climbed loudly up to her hiding place.

She twisted around just as a coil-gun appeared over the edge, followed by the face of the soldier who carried it. Price kicked at the barrel as the coil-gun fired, feeling the wind of the bullet's passage, missing her by inches. She grabbed at the barrel of the gun, then kicked again, aiming for the Bzadian's face, feeling the crunch of a broken nose. She wrenched the gun off its cable spring as he fell backward.

It was the only shot she had. It was her only chance, the only time she would have. A matter of seconds that would determine whether she lived or died, right here, right now.

In one clean movement she rolled to the front of the machine, brought the weapon to bear, and squeezed the trigger.

The shot hit the can slightly off center, the metal bullet puncturing it cleanly on both sides and punching it out of the soldier's hands. A white mist filled the room and spread through the open door into the access tube. The room filled with an eerie silence.

They found Price lying in a room full of peppermint haze, surrounded by staring Bzadian soldiers whose eyes flicked constantly and whose expressions spat hatred without a muscle moving in their faces. She had crawled toward the door but hadn't made it. She was semiconscious and retching, but alive.

"I'll go get her," the Tsar said.

"Don't be a hero," Chisnall said. "Wait till we can find a gas mask or ventilate the room. It's not safe."

"I'll go," Monster said.

"Wait . . . ," Chisnall began, but there was no arguing. From the look on Monster's face, nobody was going to stop him.

So it was Monster who held his breath and entered the corridor to the plant room while the others secured the rest of the complex, rounding up the technicians and operators and keeping them under guard in a meeting room, subduing those who tried to resist with puffer bullets and Puke spray.

And it was Monster who emerged from the corridor with Price over his large shoulders and laid her tenderly on the floor in the entrance pod, where the air was clearest. He wiped vomit from her lips, checked her vital signs, and gently stroked her forehead. When he put his ears to her lips to listen to her breathing, her hand slipped around the back of his neck and pulled him close. Monster didn't pull away.

When focus finally returned to her eyes, they were all gathered around her. The SONRAD facility was secure and the remainder of the soldiers down at the wharf had been rescued from the sea, disarmed, cuffed, and placed in the meeting room with the others.

Monster stood back as Price took in the faces that hovered over her.

"Are you okay?" Chisnall asked.

Price tried to laugh, but it came out as a cough. "Happy New Year," she said.

Chisnall checked the time. It was after midnight.

"Happy New Year, Price," he said.

BOOK 2—THE RIVER

8. OPERATION MAGNUM

FROM THE FIRST PROPOSAL TO THE TRANSPORT SHIPS arriving off the Australian coast, Operation Magnum had taken just three weeks.

The task force was made up of seventy amphibious Marine Personnel Carriers (MPCs) carrying 1,200 soldiers: US Marines, Canadian Black Devils, Russian Spetsnaz, and German Kommando Spezialkrafte. In addition, there were three British L118 artillery pieces and ten Chinese T-63a amphibious tanks (although only nine actually made it ashore).

The Bzadians had chosen Lowood as the site of the fuel-processing plant due to its proximity to the mighty Wivenhoe Dam, which provided the constant high-volume supply of both water and electricity that was vital to the production of the cells.

Experts had ruled out an attack on the dam. Wivenhoe was a huge earthen embankment, safe from anything short of a nuclear bomb. The massive metal gates, among the largest in the world, were almost indestructible and heavily defended.

Instead, the plan called for the task force to infiltrate Bzadian territory through the Brisbane River. Amphibious vehicles, mostly submerged and cloaked by an artificial mist, would have to navigate nearly a hundred miles of river in the pitch-black, without being detected. Power stations had to be knocked out. Sonar and radar had to be eliminated.

The other problem was the moon. For the operation to succeed, it would have to take place during a new moon, when the Brisbane River would be in darkness. Only one date met all the criteria: December 31, 2031.

9. SONRAD

[MISSION DAY 2]
[0020 hours local time]
[Bzadian SONRAD station, St. Helena Island, New Bzadia]

"TASK FORCE ACTUAL, THIS IS ANGEL ONE. VIPER CHANNEL is open."

"Angel One, this is Task Force Actual. Please confirm your last."

"Angel One, confirming Viper Channel is open. How copy?"

"Solid copy, Angel One, good work. Our ETA is approximately ten mikes."

Against all odds they had done it. The route into New Bzadia was open. It was only the first step on a long and precarious path, but still it gave Chisnall hope that somehow they would be able to achieve the impossible.

Monster was still tending to Price while Wilton checked out the speedboat they had seen moored at the wharf. Barnard was guarding the prisoners and the Tsar was monitoring the communications room.

Chisnall had barely finished talking to the task force command when the Tsar's voice sounded in his ear.

"Where are you, Big Dog? I got Pukes on the line."

Chisnall took a deep breath. The SONRAD complex had been off-line for less than ten minutes, but that was long enough for the local command center to investigate. He hurried to the communications room. He had been expecting the call and had already changed into the uniform of a plant operator.

"Verification key gen up and running?" he asked.

"Ready to rock and ready to roll," the Tsar said.

Chisnall punched a button on the desk. A video screen sprang to life. His momentary nervousness eased. He could pass himself off as a Bzadian. He knew that. The years of training back at Fort Carson, the surgical operations to recolor his skin, to change the shape of his skull, and to fork his tongue made certain that he looked and acted like one of them. An alien. And the disguise had been well tested in the red sands of the Australian desert.

"SONRAD communications. I am Chizel," he said.

"I am Major Zara Kriz from the Coastal Defense Command," a female said. She appeared efficient and competent. It was the same voice he had heard on board the ship, with the same slightly odd accent. He hoped she didn't recognize his voice. He tried to speak in a lower register and quickly changed his accent to one of the other Bzadian races, which had their own peculiar way of making the buzzing sound that was a feature of all Bzadian languages. It was a softer, quicker buzz, and it felt odd on his tongue, but he had practiced it many times in training.

"Where is Hez?" Kriz asked. "I was speaking to him earlier."

"Shift change," Chisnall said.

"I see. Chizel, please identify," Kriz said, making a note.

"Of course," Chisnall said, and removed one of his ID tubes, inserting it into a scanner below the video screen. It was a perfect fake.

"Confirmed," Kriz said as the tube scanned in her system. "We had an interrupted feed from SONRAD a few minutes ago."

"Our apologies," Chisnall said, covering his face briefly with his hands. "A circuit protector tripped in the electricity plant."

That was a reasonable excuse. It was also, of course, totally false. They had had to take the SONRAD facility off-line while the Tsar replaced vital circuits in the systems with ones that were programmed to ignore the task force vessels.

"And the backup power?"

"That failed under the sudden load," Chisnall said. "The techs restored it and are reviewing the backup power system to find out why it failed."

"I'll need authentication on this."

"Of course," Chisnall said. "Please send the verification codes."

A series of numbers appeared at the bottom of the screen. The Tsar punched them into the key generator and a response code appeared. Human hackers had cracked the Bzadian authentication codes many months before.

Chisnall typed the response into a keypad, and Kriz said, "Verification completed at 00:25 hours."

"Did your security teams check the ship?" Kriz asked.

"Yes, they boarded and searched it," Chisnall said. "There appeared to have been some kind of explosion. Some of the crew were injured, but not badly." He had to suppress a smile. He was being asked to verify his own lies.

"I have been trying to reach the ship again," Kriz said, "but there is no response."

Chisnall's inner smile disappeared. Of course Kriz would check back in with the ship. He should have anticipated that.

"That is strange," he said awkwardly.

"Yes," Kriz said. "Very strange. Where is your security team now?"

The Tsar stepped up behind him, into the range of the video monitor.

"We have had a report from the wharf," he said. He seemed relaxed and natural. "They have shut down the ship's power while they try to repair the equipment."

"I see. Please ask them to contact me when their radio is active again," Kriz said, making another note.

"That might be a few hours away," the Tsar said. "The damage was quite severe."

"As soon as possible, please," Kriz said.

"Of course," Chisnall said.

There was a pause; then Kriz frowned. "You are sure everything is okay?"

"Everything is fine," Chisnall said with a smile. "The radar and sonar scopes are clear. I do not think the scumbugz will try to invade today."

Kriz laughed and broke the connection.

"Think she believed us?" the Tsar asked.

"I think so," Chisnall said.

"And if she didn't?"

"We'll find out soon enough," Chisnall said, and added, "Thanks for backing me up just then."

"You didn't need me," the Tsar said. "You had everything under control."

No, I didn't, Chisnall thought. The Tsar was a fluent liar and a good actor. Too good.

Chisnall keyed his comm. "Monster, how's Price?"

"She okay," came the reply.

"Is she able to move?"

"Yes."

"Okay, everyone meet at the wharf," Chisnall said. "We're Oscar Mike in five."

10. VIPER CHANNEL

[0045 hours local time]

[Brisbane River Mouth, Brisbane, New Bzadia]

THE SPEEDBOAT CAME ASHORE AT THE PORT OF BRISBANE, drifting quietly below rusting cranes, unused since the Bzadians took over Australia. There the Angels off-loaded the rest of their equipment before pulling the bung from the boat and pushing it back offshore, where it settled and gradually sank.

Chisnall powered up his T-board, the Bzadian army's "personal transportation device." A T-shaped platform, with two ball-type wheels at the front and one at the back, it was powered by a small but silent motor. You rode it like a skateboard. Pressure from the left or right of the front foot steered the device. Pressing on the ball of the rear foot increased speed, and releasing it applied braking. The rubberized wheels were smooth and quiet. The hum of the other Angels' T-boards made a low chorus around him as they tested their boards.

The Angels had changed into standard Bzadian uniforms with markings that identified them as a security patrol. They waited on the boardwalk at a small marina, desolate and empty of the yachts and powered craft that would once have filled its long, many-jointed jetties. Chisnall tried sitting on the platform of his T-board, but that was uncomfortable, so he ended up sitting on a low grassy bank that adjoined the boardwalk. The others followed his lead, except for Wilton, who paced back and forth, burning off some nerves.

The lights of the city stained the surface of the water with a spectrum of colored bands reaching across the river toward them. Occasionally, a light breeze would ruffle the picture, scattering the tidy lines into a kaleidoscope of colored dots.

"Listen up," Chisnall said, gesturing at the river. "In a few minutes the entire task force is going to glide right by. They need to get all the way to Ipswich undetected. We're going to make sure that happens."

"We're gonna be their guardian angels," Price said.

"That's right," Chisnall said. "Any Puke shows too much interest, take him down quickly and quietly. We've got the right side of the river and the Demons are handling the left. Clear?"

"Game on," the Tsar said.

"Boo-yah," Wilton said.

"Demons had better get power off soon," Monster murmured.

Chisnall glanced back at the city. The central business district made a river of light against the night sky.

"Maybe they're waiting until the task force gets closer," he said.

"They're cutting it close," Wilton said.

Downriver, a low, light mist was spreading and settling on the water on either side of the wreck of the HMAS *Australia*. Vague shapes, low and black, the turrets of the task force vehicles, moved within the mist. Chisnall had to strain his eyes to make them out. Good. To a casual observer they would be all but invisible.

But it wouldn't be as easy when they reached the city. Not if the lights were still on.

He listened carefully, despite the machinery grinding through the water; the sound on the surface of the river was no more than a low thrum.

After the strain of the last few hours, sitting on the grassy bank by the river in the soft reflected glow of the city lights seemed peaceful, as if they were on holiday, not on a life-and-death mission. The Tsar seemed the most relaxed of all. He began to sing a highly profane song, the lyrics of which concerned the size of Bzadian genitalia.

Wilton joined in, but with little enthusiasm.

The wreck of the *Australia* had now disappeared into the unnatural mist. It reminded Chisnall of the tendrils of fog that had been creeping from the plant room back on the island. A room full of frozen Bzadian soldiers and one very sick Angel. Price seemed to have suffered no long-lasting effects, which was a relief.

Wilton had found some pebbles and was tossing them into

the water. Each splash, although soft, made Chisnall jump. He wanted to tell Wilton to stop, but that would make him seem on edge. The Tsar was checking and calibrating his scope, a handheld radar system carried by Bzadian soldiers.

"That was cool when that ship tried to bomb us and blew itself up instead," Wilton said. "How lucky was that!"

"Real lucky." Price caught Chisnall's eye, and he smiled.

"That was some pretty fancy shooting at the wharf, Wilton," Chisnall said.

"At that range it was like hitting a barn door with a shotgun," Wilton said.

"And it was pretty smart thinking, shooting the Puke spray can," Chisnall said to Price.

"Lucky shot," Price said. "Someone should invent Puke spray grenades."

"Like smoke grenades, but filled with Puke spray," the Tsar agreed. "Great idea."

"Isn't that chemical warfare?" Barnard asked. Her eyes, too, were on the mist that disguised the approaching fleet.

"What's the difference if we spray it in their faces or let off a gas grenade?" Price asked.

"There're laws against chemical warfare," Barnard said. "Otherwise, if we do it to them, next thing they're doing it to us."

"Can't shoot 'em, can't gas 'em—what do they expect us to do, hug them to death?" Wilton asked. He skimmed a pebble out across the river. It bounced once, then sank.

"Monster could fart on them," Price said.

"That still counts as chemical warfare," Chisnall said.

"Yeah, sure," the Tsar said. "We're on the verge of being wiped off the planet, but let's not break the rules." He put away the scope and lay backward on the grassy bank and shut his eyes. He appeared relaxed, but Chisnall wasn't fooled.

"We'll wipe *them* off the planet," Wilton said. "It's our frigging planet."

"Not if they get across the Bering Strait," Price said.

"We're here to make sure that doesn't happen," Chisnall said. "And it won't."

"Boo-yah," Wilton said.

"If the mission succeeds," Barnard said, staring out over the water.

"It will," Chisnall said, his jaw firmly set.

"You're sure about this?" Barnard asked, still without looking at him, or anyone.

"It has to," Chisnall said. Failure was not an option he could consider.

"It is the way things are meant to be," Monster said.

"Say what?" the Tsar said.

"Monster believes that everything happens for a reason," Price said.

"Everything happens because it happens," Barnard said. "There's no reason. There's no grand plan."

"The universe is a river flowing to its destination," Monster said. "We are merely drifting on the current."

Barnard turned to him. The first time she had looked at any of them.

"No, Monster. See that big brown thing full of water down

there? That's a river," she said, gesturing at it. "The universe is a big black thing full of stars."

"If the universe is flowing like a river," the Tsar said, "then what the hell are we doing here? If everything is predestined, then we can't change anything. We should go home and let the universe get on with it."

Wilton tossed a larger stone into the river and they watched as the ripples spread, then dissipated.

"It'd be a lot less aggravation," Price said.

"Every one of us who puts a toe in a river changes the flow of the water, just slightly," Monster said.

"Did he get dropped on his head at Uluru?" the Tsar asked.

Chisnall laughed, but the Tsar wasn't wrong. Monster had changed since Uluru. They had all changed.

The mist was almost upon them now, although it was confined to the middle of the river, pouring from tubes atop the MPCs.

"Time to get our toes wet," Chisnall said.

"Where the hell are those goddamn Demons?" Price muttered, and as if on cue, the lights in the city went out. The tall buildings on either side of the river, which had been lit in a thousand tiny square patches, were now silhouettes, black against the black of the sky.

The river, which had seemed to pulse with an internal life force, now seemed dead—a snaky void ensnared by the banks that rose on either side.

As the first of the vehicles reached their position, Chisnall stood and powered up his T-board again.

"We are Oscar Mike," he said softly. "The front door is open. Let's see if we can keep it that way."

In the Coastal Defense Center in the old Victoria Barracks building, Major Zara Kriz debated with herself whether to raise the alert level, putting ready reaction forces on standby, or to wait for more information. Raising the alert level would get several high-ranking officers out of bed, and the first thing they would ask her was why.

And to tell the truth, she didn't know why. An accident on a ship. A power outage at the SONRAD station. A loss of communication with the ship. All had perfectly reasonable explanations, but added together they started to create a disturbing picture.

She decided to question Chizel, the operator at the SONRAD station, a little more thoroughly. That might set her mind at rest. Kriz punched the buttons on her video screen to place the call.

The Bzadian city slept, but it was not dead, and, as with human cities, there seemed to be a wide range of Bzadians who needed to be out and about in the middle of the night. Delivery trucks passed, splashing them with light, the drivers completely unaware of the six human teenagers in Bzadian army uniforms who prowled through the heart of the city.

"Demon One, this is Angel One. How copy?" Chisnall said.

The comm channel crackled into life. "Hey, Varmint, there's noises on the baby monitor," a voice said.

"Status check, Demon One," Chisnall said with a sigh.

"All clear over here," Varmint said. "Nine Pukes down, and counting. What's your score?"

Chisnall shut his eyes and drew a deep breath. This was the first time they had undertaken a combined mission with the Demons, and he was finding he didn't really like their way of doing things.

"It's not a contest, Varmint, and if you leave a trail of bodies behind you, somebody might stumble over one. Only take them out if there's no other way. You know the rules of engagement."

"So y'all are way behind." Varmint laughed. "Don't worry, you still got time."

The Tsar broke in, imitating and exaggerating Varmint's Southern accent. "By golly, Varmint, I guess y'all must be better than us at this kind of thing. We'll jes' watch what y'all are doing and try to learn something."

"Get back to your mission, all of you," Chisnall said.

"Someone's getting cranky," Varmint said.

Chisnall flicked off the channel, gritting his teeth in frustration. Possibly the most important mission of the war and the Demons seemed to think it was some kind of joke.

"We're never going to win this war with morons like that on our side," the Tsar said.

"Don't worry about them," Chisnall said. "Concentrate on

our part of the mission. We're in the heart of enemy territory. From now on we walk like Pukes, we talk like Pukes, we think like Pukes."

"We eat like Pukes," Wilton added.

"We fart like Pukes." Monster grinned.

"That too," Chisnall said.

"If we could think like Pukes, this war would already be over," Barnard said, almost to herself.

Kriz hung up the phone and clasped her hands to stop herself from rubbing at the skin on her arm, which was turning red and rough.

There had been no reply at the SONRAD station.

Could it be somehow due to the blackout? A failure at an electricity substation had caused a ripple effect that had taken down the entire power grid? But SONRAD had backup power. Unless it had failed again.

And while she was trying to contact SONRAD, a call had come in from a restaurant owner. Nanzi, one of her staff, had put it through.

It had been alarming, to say the least. The restaurateur had been heading home when he had noticed something odd in the river. Whatever it was, it had worried him enough to call the Coastal Defense Command.

Her office was only a five-minute walk from one of the bridges that spanned the river, and Kriz had arranged to meet him there. There were too many strange things going on. She was sure that something was seriously wrong, if only she could put her finger on what it was.

Asking Nanzi to cover for her for a few minutes, she checked that her phone was working, worried that the power outage might have affected the phone network. She dialed Nanzi's phone and was relieved to hear the sound of ringing. The cellular system they had inherited from the humans operated on its own backup power supply.

She drew a sidearm and a set of night-vision goggles from the armory and set off for the bridge.

The T-board hummed under Chisnall's feet, his speed steady at twenty miles per hour, according to the GPS on his wrist computer. His coil-gun was holstered on his back, and his Puke spray was ready on his utility belt. He scanned the buildings on both sides of the river, watching for any sign of life, for any interest in the river.

A vehicle turned a corner, spotlighting the team for a moment—like escaping prisoners against the wall of a jail—before sweeping on. Traffic was otherwise light, pedestrians were few, and the buildings around them were silent and still. Even so, Chisnall had the sense that a thousand eyes, in a thousand darkened windows, were staring at the river.

"This is really creepy," Wilton said in an eerie echo of Chisnall's thoughts.

"You got that right," Price said.

"Meh, this is nothing," the Tsar said.

"Here we go," Price said.

"In Japan we had to recon through dense forest," the Tsar said. "There could have been an ambush behind every tree, a booby trap under every step."

"Gosh, that sounds dangerous. Did you survive?" Barnard asked, wide-eyed.

The Tsar ignored her. "What I did then, and what I'm doing now, is to focus every sense. I'm listening, noticing even the tiniest sound. I'm smelling things. My eyes are scanning every object in my vicinity, evaluating it as a possible threat."

"And I guess the scope helps," Price said.

"I can smell something right now," Barnard said. "Bull."

Again, the Tsar didn't rise to the bait. "Try it," he said.

"Oh, I'm trying," Price said. "I'm listening as hard as I can, but all I can hear is you yapping."

The Tsar was silent at that, and for all their scorn, Chisnall found the Tsar was right. Once you were aware of it, the air was full of sound. The sound of truck engines reverberating off city blocks. The dull burr of the task force beneath the waters of the river. Overhead, the harsh caws of parakeets and crows and the screech of fruit bats. There were smells too. More than he had realized. This close to the river there was an odor of muddy water, tinged with decay.

The Tsar didn't stay silent for long. "There was one time—"

"Shut up, Tsar," the others said in unison.

■ ■ ■

The concrete path they were following took a sharp turn away from the river. Ahead of them was a grassy park, dotted with shrubs. Chisnall led the way into the park, wanting to stay by the river's edge.

Bzadians didn't celebrate the human New Year, but the two Bzadian teenagers here were locked in a celebration all of their own.

Chisnall's rifle leaped into his arms at the sight of two figures appearing from a dip in the ground, seemingly from nowhere, but he relaxed and reholstered it as the two, awkward and embarrassed, tried to rearrange their clothing and act as though they were just out for an evening stroll.

Chisnall sent them on their way with a short admonition, reflecting that a lot of human kids in the Free Territories were probably up to much the same thing that night. The young Bzadian female giggled as they disappeared into the nearby streets, hand in hand, and for a moment Chisnall felt even more keenly the weight that was pressing on his shoulders.

"How sweet," the Tsar said.

"Not when they're Pukes," Wilton said.

"Even when they're Pukes," the Tsar said.

Barnard snorted.

"Never been in love, huh, Barnard?" the Tsar said.

"Love?" Barnard said. "No such thing. It's merely a convenience for society."

"You'd make a good Bzadian," Price said. "That's how they think."

"Don't worry, Barnard, there's still time for you," the Tsar said. "There's still hope."

"Not with you there's not," Barnard said.

"We've got a tail," Wilton said as they emerged from the park back onto pavement.

Chisnall looked around to see a dog running along behind them in the middle of the roadway.

"Well, *it's* got a tail," Wilton said. He slowed and extended a hand back to it. "Nice, doggie."

The dog growled, a deep, feral sound.

"Or not," Wilton said, increasing his speed.

The dog could have been a Labrador but had longish fur. Maybe a mixed breed, Chisnall thought. It had gentle eyes, completely at odds with the harsh growl it had given Wilton. It ran beside them, tongue hanging out of its mouth as they rolled along the roadway, but disappeared as they veered onto a bike path that followed the riverbank.

Chisnall stared down at the river. The task force was a dark mass, shrouded by the man-made mist, which persisted, despite the indecisive breeze tearing short-lived holes in it. Only the turrets of the vehicles protruded out of the water, black against the black of the river, and with its blanket of mist, the fleet was very difficult to detect unless you knew it was there.

"See how clean the streets are?" Price said.

Chisnall hadn't noticed until Price pointed it out. "No litter," he said.

"No chewing gum," Price said.

"Yeah, and I bet they always signal their turns and wash

their hands after they sneeze," the Tsar said. "They'd be real nice folk if they hadn't started a war."

"Did they?" Barnard asked.

"Did they what?" the Tsar asked.

"Start the war," Barnard said.

"What do you mean?" Wilton asked. "Everybody knows what happened in 2020."

"Don't believe everything you read in books," Barnard said.

"Dog's back," Wilton said.

This time it was in front of them, having taken some secret shortcut that maybe only dogs knew. It sat in the middle of the bike path and didn't move as they approached.

They slowed.

The dog growled, that same low vicious sound from the back of its throat.

"Everybody hold up," Chisnall said. There was little choice. The dog stood, blocking the path, its ears back, its teeth bared.

Wilton hopped off his T-board and advanced slowly toward the animal. "Good boy," he said in English. "Good boy."

"Don't use English," Chisnall said.

The dog let him get within about five feet before lunging forward, snarling, only backing off as Wilton's coil-gun swung over his shoulder into his hands.

Chisnall found his own weapon in his hands. He hadn't realized he had hit the release. The action had become instinctive.

Wilton backed away. "I don't think it likes me," he said.

Strings of drool hung from the dog's jowls as it bared its teeth even more, refusing to give ground.

"I don't think it likes any of us," the Tsar said.

"It's probably never smelled a human before," Barnard said.

"Shoot it," Price said.

"With a puffer?" Wilton asked.

"Is just a dog," Monster said. "Leave him alone."

"It's not a him," Barnard said. "It's a girl."

"Gotta do something," Chisnall said. "It's going to draw attention to us."

He glanced up at the apartment windows that overlooked the path.

"Is just being dog," Monster said. He walked past Wilton, unhooking his coil-gun as he went. He held the gun out with both hands, barrel first.

The dog snarled and barked as he approached.

"I got a couple of vehicles on the scope, coming this way," the Tsar said. "Could be a security patrol."

"Shut the bloody thing up," Price said. "Or I'll do it." She drew her knife.

"Don't touch the dog," Monster said. "Is beautiful animal."

"And it's in our way," Price said.

"Don't touch the dog!" Monster raised his voice.

It was the first time Chisnall had ever seen him angry. Price hesitated but sheathed her knife. "Then hurry the puke up," she said.

Monster advanced on the dog. It half lunged at him a couple of times but pulled back as he kept the barrel of the weapon in between them.

Slowly, he moved forward, forcing the dog off to the side

of the bike path. "Now go," he said to Chisnall with a jerk of his head. He kept the dog trapped against the railing until the others were past, then backed away.

The dog followed, snarling and growling but not attacking.

"What's the story with that patrol?" Chisnall asked.

"Heading away from us for now," the Tsar said. "They're following the highway east along the river."

"Okay, keep moving. Maybe that mutt will give up and go find something else to do."

Glancing at the river, he saw that the mist that blanketed the Task Force had not yet reached this point. "Everybody hold here for two mikes," he said. "Give the Task Force a chance to catch up."

The dog stopped when they stopped, maintaining a careful distance.

Without warning, Barnard, just in front of Chisnall, dropped to one knee and released her weapon. She scanned a high balcony through the telescopic sight. Chisnall trained his own sight on the balcony but could see no movement.

Barnard stood and reholstered her weapon. All without a word.

"See something?" Chisnall asked.

"It was nothing. Just some clothes," she said.

"You're sure?"

"Yeah."

"What did you mean before about thinking like Pukes?" he asked.

"It doesn't matter," Barnard said.

"It might," Chisnall said.

His last sergeant, Holly Brogan, had understood how Bzadians thought. A little too well.

Barnard shrugged. "They don't think like us. We can't beat them if we don't understand them."

Chisnall said, "We can't beat them if we don't have the right strategy."

"That's what I'm saying," Barnard said. "Strategy is psychology."

"And you've studied strategy?" the Tsar asked.

"No, but I've studied psychology," Barnard said. "We keep using strategies and tactics that have worked against humans. If we thought like Pukes, this war would already be over."

"I suppose you understand the way they think," Price said.

"Better than most," Barnard said.

"How do you mean?" Wilton asked. "How is strategy like psychology?"

"Strategy is the art of outthinking the enemy by understanding how they will react," Barnard said.

"Like how?" Wilton asked.

"Like the Second World War . . ." Barnard paused and looked back at Wilton. "You have heard of the Second World War?"

Wilton flipped her the bird.

"Just checking," Barnard said. "In 1940, Britain was on the verge of defeat. Hitler wanted to invade but couldn't because of the RAF, the Royal Air Force. So he told the Luftwaffe to bomb the RAF out of existence. It almost worked. A few more weeks and Britain would have had no effective air force."

"So why didn't Hitler finish them off?" Price asked.

"Psychology," Barnard said. "Churchill, Britain's leader at the time, ordered bombing raids on Berlin. Hitler was enraged. He ordered the Luftwaffe to attack British cities in retaliation. The airfields were left alone. The RAF was able to recover. The invasion of Britain was delayed and eventually canceled."

"But because of Churchill's decision," Chisnall said, "hundreds of thousands of civilians were killed."

"Strategies have consequences," Barnard said. "Churchill did what he had to do."

He did what he had to do, Chisnall thought. Or was that just a phrase for avoiding the blame for something terrible? Like Uluru?

"What if you had to make a decision like that, and it meant that all of us would get killed?" Price asked. "Would you do it?"

"Of course. I wouldn't even have to think about it," Barnard said.

"You're no fun," Wilton said.

"What about you, LT?" Barnard said.

She was watching him. Evaluating him. Her eyes were focused like laser beams, cutting through any defenses, seeing right inside him.

"I'd do whatever it took to get the job done," he said, and wondered if it was true.

A round of furious barking from the dog brought

movement in a second-story window. Chisnall's hand strayed to his gun release.

"Anybody got eyes on the gray building at two o'clock?" he asked. "Second floor, window to the right."

"Female with a baby," Wilton replied immediately. "I've been watching them since we stopped."

"Okay, take it easy," he said. "Only take her down if you absolutely have to. We don't want her dropping the baby."

"I don't think she's noticed us," Wilton said. "The baby seems upset. I think she's just trying to calm it down."

Even so, they remained a moment until the Bzadian female disappeared from the window.

"Whatever it takes, huh, Chisnall?" Barnard said.

Chisnall said nothing.

"That patrol has turned around," the Tsar said. "Now heading west, coming this way."

"Okay. We need to get out of sight," Chisnall said.

"There's a patch of trees up here on the right," Wilton said. "Just past the bridge."

"How long have we got, Tsar?" Chisnall asked.

"A couple of minutes," the Tsar said.

The trees were on the bank of the river, below the bike path. To get to them they had to climb the low fence of the bike path and jump down to the ground. The trees were thick and leafy, providing ample protection from view.

The dog, however, stopped, right alongside their position, and began to bark at them through the railings of the fence.

"Somebody shut that dog up," Chisnall said.

The dog was barking madly now, lunging against the railings.

"I'll do it," Price said.

"No, I do it," Monster said. "She will listen to me."

"Sixty seconds," the Tsar said.

A low growling came from Monster's throat and the dog stopped barking as it pondered this new development.

"Just as well he speaks its language," Wilton said.

"They're probably related," Price said.

Monster reached up to the fence and hauled himself back up onto the bike path. The dog backed away as he approached, then started barking again, louder and louder.

"Thirty seconds," the Tsar said.

"Shut that mutt up," Chisnall said.

"Shhh," Monster said. He advanced, and the dog retreated, jumping and growling. They moved out of sight.

"Shhh." They heard Monster's voice gently now on the comm. "Shhh."

The dog barked again, then stopped.

"Shhh," Monster said.

After that there was silence.

"How'd he do that?" Barnard asked.

Chisnall smiled. "He loves animals. He has a real way with them."

"Patrol's right on us," the Tsar said, and they all heard the engine of the Land Rover as it passed along the highway on the other side of the trees. Almost as quickly, it was gone, the sound fading into the distance.

They waited for Monster, who appeared a moment later, not up on the bike path, but through the trees, from the bank of the river.

"Where's the dog?" Chisnall asked.

"Gone," Monster said. "Gone home. I think."

There was something hard in his eyes.

"What did you do?" Chisnall asked quietly.

Barnard snorted. "What do you think he did?"

"Monster?" Chisnall asked.

Monster was silent, unmoving.

"He wouldn't have hurt the dog," Chisnall said. "Would you, Monster?"

"Of course not," Monster said.

"Of course not," Chisnall said. "Now let's get out of here before the task force gets too far ahead of us."

11. MAN DOWN

[0135 hours local time]
[Bzadian Coastal Defense Command, Brisbane, New Bzadia]

ON THE ROAD TO THE BRIDGE, KRIZ STOPPED AND STARED at the river. Her NV goggles revealed a low, dense mist. Something seemed odd about the river. The restaurateur had mentioned boats on the phone, but she couldn't see any, unless they were very low in the water.

Then it clicked. The *mist* was what was odd. There was often a mist on the surface of the river, but that was in winter, when cold air reacted with warmer water. In summer, a mist was unusual, if not impossible, she thought.

A slight movement of the mist revealed a flicker of a dark shadow. Or was that just her imagination, coloring in the outline that the restaurateur had given her?

Intrigued, and more than a little alarmed, she continued to walk toward the bridge. Despite the recent odd occurrences, she could not bring herself to believe this was some kind of enemy activity. The radar and sonar feeds from the SONRAD station were still fully operational. They would have picked up any enemy forces the moment they entered the bay, well before they got anywhere near the river. The power blackout, however, was a worrying coincidence. She checked the time as she took her first step onto the bridge so she could log it later. It was 01:40 hours.

"What you said about us starting the war, you really think that's true?" Chisnall asked, off comm, coasting up alongside Barnard.

"Some people believe it," Barnard said.

"And you?"

Barnard swerved away from him to avoid a cracked area of concrete that had risen up to form a small ridge.

"I'm open-minded."

"Nice to know," Chisnall said, letting a cold chill drop into his voice. "But you can keep it to yourself from now on. These guys don't need to have doubts about why they're putting their lives on the line here."

"I don't get you, Chisnall," Barnard said. "I'm trying to figure you out and I'm failing."

"Don't worry about it. Just stay on task," Chisnall said.

"I don't care what people think of me," Barnard said. "Price ignores me. Wilton is terrified of me. I don't care about the Tsar. He's a jerk. And Monster doesn't talk much anyway. But you? You're a mystery to me."

"How so?"

"Because these guys all look up to you like you're some kind of god. But all I see is a scared little boy."

"Ouch," Chisnall said.

"What these guys need is a leader who's not afraid to lead," Barnard said.

"You don't pull your punches, do you?" Chisnall said.

"I heard about Uluru," Barnard said. "Get over it. Stop trying to protect these guys and start doing your job."

"I am doing my job," Chisnall said. "You keep your ideas to yourself. These guys don't need to be wondering whose side you're really on."

She turned to face him and her eyes were stony. "I'm no traitor," she said.

"Then what are you?" Chisnall asked. "The most important mission of the war and they landed me with you. No combat history, no explanations. I could have used another experienced soldier."

"Like the Hero of Hokkaido?" Barnard said with a small twist of a smile.

"Yes, like the Tsar. But I got you," Chisnall said. "Someone who knows things they're not supposed to know. Who are you?"

"That's not important," Barnard said.

"I'll decide that," Chisnall said.

"It's above your security level, Lieutenant," Barnard said.

"I'm in command of this team," Chisnall said. "Right here, right now, nothing is above my security level."

"This is," Barnard said.

Chisnall opened his mouth, but any further questions would have to wait. A Bzadian came running out of a side street, right at them.

"Help! Help!" He was not in uniform. He was a civilian, which, to a human, was a rare sight. The interactions humans had with Bzadians were mostly at the end of a gun.

"The river!" the civilian said.

He was overweight, also an unusual state for a Bzadian. His fingers were soft and pudgy and even the short run over to their position left him breathless. His hands waved around like windmills.

"What is it, sir?" Chisnall asked.

"There's something in the river!" the Bzadian puffed.

"River monsters, perhaps?" Price asked.

"Boats!" the Bzadian said. "Small boats. I think they're sc—" He couldn't bring himself to say the word. "The enemy!"

"Scumbugz?" Chisnall asked. "Here in the middle of New Bzadia? That's not possible."

"I know what I saw," the fat Bzadian said.

"Have you alerted the Coastal Defense Command?" Chisnall asked.

"Yes."

"All right, we'll check it out," Chisnall said. "But in the meantime I want you to let us know if you see anyone carrying cans of Puke spray."

"Puke spray?" The Bzadian seemed even more alarmed. "What is it?"

"Like this," Chisnall said, and showed him.

Monster caught the Bzadian as he slumped, then effortlessly slung the flabby shape over one shoulder.

"Put him somewhere he won't be found," Chisnall said. He looked at the others. "I think we may have a problem."

"Movement up ahead," Wilton said.

Kris stopped about a quarter of the way across the bridge and leaned over the rail to peer down. Something was floating beneath the mist. Whatever it was, it was large, ripples spreading backward down the river as far as she could see. There was an unusual sound in the air also, a low murmur that seemed to be coming from the water.

She reached for her phone, but even as she did, a realization struck her. The restaurateur. Where was he? He had said he would meet her on the bridge. Had something happened to him? If so, was she in danger too? She glanced around the bridge, seeing nothing, then down at the bike path, which ran along the riverbank. A vague blur of movement caught her eye. She dropped just as a thud hit the rail above her. A mist of fine gray powder wafted downward. Instinctively, she shut her eyes and mouth and clamped two fingers over her nose, rolling out onto the roadway as another thud sounded.

Something was wrong with her vision now—the images in the NV goggles were swimming, and when she tried to stand up, her legs were weak and loose. Dark figures were scrambling over median barriers onto the bridge on-ramp. She tried to focus on them but her eyes were a blur.

On her hands and knees, she scurried away from them—away from her command center and safety.

Her command center. In the fog of her brain, she remembered her phone.

She peered at the buttons, but they were just blurs. Kriz forced her eyes to focus and pressed the speed-dial button. A voice answered. It was someone she knew well, although she could not remember his name. She tried to talk through thick lips but her tongue was a swollen, useless lump of meat and only groaning sounds emerged.

Now there were dark figures running up the bridge toward her. There was no time. Somehow, she got to her feet and staggered to the railing of the bridge, leaning over, and over. The mist below her looked like a soft cushion for her fall, but that was an illusion. The truth was the cold hardness of the river water.

The shock gave Kriz clarity. Her eyes began to focus; her tongue began to stir. But the phone was gone, knocked from her grasp by the impact. Her NV goggles had somehow remained in place and the river was a dark green otherworld.

The current dragged her downstream, and she began to flail back to the surface, desperate for a gasp of air. She watched in astonishment as a giant black fish swam toward her . . . no, not a fish, a tank. A human battle tank, floating beneath the surface, its huge treads idle yet terrifying as they passed inches from her face.

Tanks, floating in the river! Kriz had no time to comprehend the meaning of this discovery as she reached the surface and gasped in a lungful of air, then another. Vaguely, through the mist, she could make out the bridge. Figures were bending over the railing. They must have seen her too. Guns swung in her direction. She plunged back below the surface as bullets disintegrated in the water around her.

"Where the hell is he?" Chisnall yelled.

"Can't see him in the mist!" Price yelled back.

"Anyone got eyes on?" Chisnall asked. No one replied. "Well, keep looking."

"Maybe he's unconscious," the Tsar said. "Wilton's shot was right by his face."

"No such luck," Price said. "You don't breathe in puffer dust and keep walking."

"Maybe he fell off the bridge," the Tsar said.

"No, he definitely climbed over the railing," Wilton said.

"Find him," Chisnall said.

Before he raises the alarm. Before he puts the entire mission in jeopardy.

Deep in the river, another vehicle was approaching: a troop carrier with large bulbous wheels. Only the tops of the vehicles were above the water, Kriz realized. The rest was hidden from Bzadian eyes beneath the surface of the river.

Her mind was finally clear, freed from the effects of the few grains of the powder she had ingested. This was an invasion. No question about it, and the scale of it she could only guess at. What mattered now was raising the alarm.

She swam underwater for a few yards and then surfaced for another breath, ducking back down before the watching shooters could see her through the mist. Another vehicle loomed through the water, and, with a purpose born of desperation, she swam for it, scrabbling for a handhold. A series of rungs ran up the side and she grabbed at one, her hand slipping, then fastening firmly. The rung yanked at her arm, dragging her along with the vehicle as it made its way upriver. She clutched at a higher rung, then another, hauling herself up until her face emerged from the water. Here, right above one of the vehicles, the mist was thickest.

The shadow of the bridge passed overhead and still she held on, waiting for the pylons of the next bridge, the railway bridge.

When the sky darkened for a second time, she let go of the rung and swam to the nearest pylon. Her hands scrabbled for purchase on the rough concrete of the pylon as she worked her way around, still underwater, emerging on the upriver side, out of sight of her pursuers. A few deep breaths and she dived back under, kicking for the next pylon. From the second pylon to the riverbank was a short swim, and she emerged in a clump of bushes below the bridge.

Kriz rested while she tried to get her breath and her bearings. She tried to think but lucid thoughts were like ghosts in the night, slipping away as she tried to latch on to them.

Only slowly did reason start to return. When it did, there was a problem.

She was on the wrong bank. Disorientated in the water, she had ended up on the far side away from her command center.

"There he is!" Barnard shouted. "By the base of the railway bridge."

The others raced over and stared down at the tiny figure on the far side of the river, clambering out of the water.

"He swam upstream against the current!" Chisnall said.

"Or hitched a ride," Barnard said. "That's what I would have done."

Chisnall glanced sideways at Barnard. The rest of them had been scanning the river downstream, waiting for the Bzadian to emerge from the water. Only Barnard had crossed the bridge to look upstream.

Wilton's rifle sounded, just a soft *phut,* right by Chisnall's ear, and puffer powder exploded on the Bzadian's back. He staggered but kept going.

"Just give me one real bullet," Wilton raged. "Just one full metal jacket and this is over right now."

"Price, Wilton, on me," Chisnall said. "We'll take care of this. You others, get back to the north bank and continue the patrol."

Chisnall leaped onto his T-board and stamped on the speed switch. It shot forward, and he nearly lost his balance, crouching down to regain it.

He looked back to see Price and Wilton close behind him.

The Demons were arrayed on the far side of the bridge.

"You lost a Puke?" Yobbo called out as they approached.

"You need us to sort it out for you?" Miscreant asked.

"We'll clean up our own mess," Chisnall said, dodging around a couple of the Demons, who didn't even try to get out of his way.

"Send a boy to do a man's job," he heard one of the Demons call out behind him.

Chisnall scanned to his right as he raced down the road and caught a glimpse of their prey, running full speed on a side road in the shadow of the railway bridge. A haze of light from a delivery truck blocked his view, and then they were past the side road and the glimpse was gone.

Chisnall tried to picture the area. They had studied a map of it many times in preparation for the mission. That side road led to a pedestrian bridge.

"I think he's trying to get back across the river," Chisnall said.

At the end of the road, a looping curve led to the left. Chisnall took it at speed, leaning into the curve, the tires protesting but holding. He had to take the curve a little wide to get around without spinning out but just managed to keep his balance. He looked around to see if Price and Wilton had kept up with him. To his surprise, they were both just ahead of him, having taken the curve slightly tighter and shooting up on the inside. The road took them around the front of the old state library and past the art gallery, now stocked with Bzadian artworks—the original human artworks, many of them priceless, left to rot in Dumpsters outside.

The parking lot of the gallery led them to a path that ran down to the pedestrian bridge, but already Chisnall could see that he had made a mistake. The bridge was empty.

"Split up," he said. "Find him."

Kriz had never intended to use the exposed pedestrian bridge, which offered no concealment. Her plan was to get up onto the railway overpass that curved above the buildings of the city.

The overpass sloped down to ground level just a few blocks away, and if she could get to that, she felt she could make it across the river, hidden behind the high metal walls of the railway bridge.

Passing a construction site, Kriz slipped past the safety barriers and trotted quickly down a footpath beside the roadwork. The machines, the equipment, and even the safety gear the road crew used were sitting in the middle of the road, waiting for work to resume the next day. The thought crossed her mind that in a human society, it would have all been locked away, to avoid the risk of it being stolen. But in the more developed, civilized Bzadian society, stealing was almost unheard of.

She crossed the street and picked up a safety helmet. One of the crew had left behind a jacket. It was a nondescript gray, a perfect cover for her uniform. She put it on, although it was at least a size too large, and picked up a tool. After hefting it a couple of times, she discarded it as too heavy and likely to slow her down. A laser-measuring meter, about the size of a flashlight, was much lighter and easier to carry. She tucked her sidearm into a pocket and slowed her gait, trudging forward. To watching eyes she would be just a weary road worker, heading home after a long shift. It occurred to her that she was stealing, like a human, but she wasn't. Not really. She would return the equipment as soon as she was able.

What was going on? Her mind was clearer now but still thoughts collided with each other, making little sense. She forced herself to calm down and try to find a rational explanation for what she had seen.

An armada of fighting vehicles was making its way up the river, destination unknown. Enemy vehicles. They were using the river to infiltrate a force into Bzadian territory. She tried to think of possible targets. The army base at Enoggera? Or the air base at Amberley? She discarded her own headquarters as a target. They had already passed that.

Someone was chasing her. They had to be humans too; nothing else made sense. They must be somehow connected to what was happening in the river. Above her, the tall concrete trusses of the railway overpass began to slope down to the ground. A wire fence blocked access to the railway tracks.

It was high, but she was pretty sure she could climb it.

"Easy does it," Chisnall said. Wilton had screamed past on a side street and Chisnall was immediately conscious that they were drawing attention to themselves.

He eased the pressure on the ball of his foot, slowing his own T-board down to a fast walking pace. "You're on patrol, not in a race."

"Copy that," Wilton's voice came back over the comm.

A road worker was ambling down a side street, away from a construction site. A female in a large jacket, wearing a helmet and carrying some kind of equipment. She didn't concern him. With any luck she would be half-asleep after a hard night's work. And he was just a soldier on patrol.

It seemed they had been lucky so far. The Bzadian from the bridge hadn't managed to raise the alarm. If he had, there would be hovering rotorcraft and heavily armed Land Rovers racing around the city.

If this were a residential area, the Bzadian could bang on a door until somebody woke up, but this part of the city was industrial, and the buildings were empty and locked.

Chisnall turned a corner, then another, circling around a city block. The next brought him onto the side road and he saw the road worker again, approaching a high metal security fence that separated the railway from the roadway. He slowed, not wanting to appear suspicious or in too much of a hurry.

You're a Bzadian soldier on patrol, he told himself. Just smile and nod.

The road worker saw him as he entered the street. She turned in his direction, waving her arms. She was clearly upset about something.

■ ■ ■

A soldier patrolling on a T-board rounded a corner just as Kriz reached the high fence. *At last! Thank Azoh! Someone with a radio.* She glanced around and then began to run toward the soldier, wanting to shout but afraid the humans, somewhere in the vicinity, would hear her.

The road worker began to run. Chisnall slowed. Best to hear what she had to say. He stopped as she ran up to him.

"Soldier," she said, "I am Major—" Her voice broke off. "Chiznel?"

It was simultaneous. The spark of recognition. The flash of understanding.

Chisnall just had time to notice wet clothes beneath an ill-fitting jacket before his eyes met her face. This was no road worker. It was Kriz, the Coastal Defense Command officer he had met via the video screen on the island. There could only be one explanation for that.

He grabbed at the can of Puke spray on his belt. She reached inside her jacket pocket. He was fast.

She was faster.

Kriz did not bother to draw the sidearm out of the jacket. That would have taken time. Her thumb found the safety catch and her finger found the trigger all in one movement. She saw the shock on Chizel's face as she fired through the fabric at point-blank range at the largest body mass, his torso.

The sound of the shot reverberated from the high walls of the buildings around her, but she didn't hesitate. Bzadian body armor was designed to shatter, to absorb the shock of a bullet by spreading the impact through the material of the armor. One shot could not penetrate. Kriz fired again as Chizel fell backward. A canister fell from his nerveless hand.

His T-board idled on the road and she grabbed it, throwing it over the fence before discarding the helmet and ill-fitting jacket and starting to climb. Others would be coming. Kriz had to get away before they got here.

The metal rails of the track were too narrow for the T-board and the center of the tracks was a series of wooden planks. But the shoulder was smooth concrete. She jumped on the T-board and jammed her toes down on the speed control. Crouching, she hoped to keep out of sight behind the metal wall of the railway overpass.

Just for a moment the danger was forgotten. At school she had been a champion T-board racer, and the rush of the wind in her hair, the hum of the wheels, and the ground flashing by brought back the thrill of the races.

Nothing made sense. Chizel had been on the island. Now Chizel was here. Something bad must have happened on the island, and now a flotilla of human vehicles was infiltrating her city. But Chizel was a Bzadian, not a human. Why would a Bzadian attack the SONRAD station? Why would a Bzadian assist a human invasion? Why would a Bzadian try to kill her?

There was something else going on here and she had to get

to the bottom of it. But her first priority was to get back to the command center and raise the alarm.

The wheels of the T-board ran across the concrete of the bridge at full speed, sprinting toward the northern bank, toward safety. Wind ruffled her hair, and her calf muscles were beginning to ache, but it was a good ache.

"Azoh! Chisnall's down!" Price yelled. She had raced to the sound of the shots and found him lying in the street, blood seeping out from beneath his body armor. He was conscious but gasping for air.

"LT?!" she cried, jumping off her T-board and sliding down on one knee beside him.

Wilton arrived just after she did. "Skipper, you okay?"

"I'm fine," Chisnall managed. "I'll be all right."

Price watched the blood soaking Chisnall's battle tunic and thought that he was wrong. Very wrong. But she said, "Looks minor, just a graze. You'll be fine."

Wilton opened his mouth but caught her eye and shut it again.

"Get after her," Chisnall managed in a voice with no air.

Her! So it was a female, Price thought. Her hands fought with the clasps of the body armor.

"The railway bridge. Get after her, Price!" Chisnall said.

Price stood. "Stay with him, Wilton," she said. "Monster, get over here. Come to Wilton's location. Chisnall's down. He's . . . Oscar Kilo . . . but you should take a look."

"On my way," Monster said.

The "Oscar Kilo" was for Chisnall's benefit, but her tone made it clear that she wanted Monster to get the heck over there right now.

She ran for the metal fence and threw her T-board over it, then leaped up, grabbed the top of the fence, and swung herself over. "Barnard, Tsar, the target is on the railway bridge, heading in your direction. See if you can get to the end of the bridge and cut her off."

"On it," the Tsar said.

Kriz was nearly halfway over the bridge when she glanced back to see another soldier, on another T-board, crest the slope on the overpass behind her.

She crouched lower, grasping the front of the board as she had done so many years ago. Whoever was behind her would not be able to catch up. She risked another look back. Her pursuer was also crouched, gripping the front of the board, either imitating her stance or an experienced racer. Kriz crouched even lower, willing the end of the bridge to arrive and with it the downward slope that would give her even more speed.

A signal box blocked the path ahead. No problem. Kriz jumped the board up onto the railing, sliding sideways with sparks flying from underneath, then leaped back onto the path on the other side.

The end of the bridge approached, and she picked up speed, shooting through a tunnel beneath a major roadway.

Incredibly, the rider behind her was gaining. *That soldier might be younger and lighter,* Kriz thought. *But I still have a trick or two up my sleeve.*

"It hurts," Chisnall said, although the truth was that the pain was gradually reducing, sinking into a dark pool inside his brain. He didn't think that was a good thing.

"You're fine, LT," Wilton said. If it was the Tsar who said it, Chisnall might have believed him. The Tsar was a much more convincing liar.

Monster spun around the corner on his T-board, dismounted, and ran over to where Chisnall lay. He began to undo Chisnall's shattered armor.

"Hey, Monster," Chisnall managed in small gasps. "How's it looking?"

"Just a scratch, I think," Monster said.

He wasn't a good liar either.

"So is this the universe's grand plan?" Chisnall asked, each word a mammoth effort.

Monster laughed. "For everything bad that happens to you," he said, "equal amount of good will come."

"Then it's gotta be a walk in the park from now on," Wilton said. "Because this mission has been a real bummer from the get-go."

"If you focus only on the bad, then you will not always see the good," Monster said.

"LT, I think we need a new Monster," Wilton said. "This one's faulty."

Monster was exploring Chisnall's chest. When he took his hands away, they were bright red with blood.

"Where are you guys?" Price yelled.

"On our way," Barnard replied.

"On your way is not good enough," Price said. "Get over here now!"

She bounced her T-board up onto the railway track, as she had seen the Bzadian do, in order to bypass the signal box. It was no different than riding a skateboard and she had been doing that almost since she could walk. The T-board skidded sideways for half a second as she landed, nearly toppling her, but she corrected and planted her foot hard on the speed control.

Now she was on the downward slope. Ahead of her the Bzadian disappeared into the gloom under a roadway. Price hit the release for her coil-gun and sprayed a volley of shots at the Bzadian, but quickly decided that firing at a moving target from a moving platform only worked in the movies. The shots were wild, and it was slowing her down.

"How's Chisnall?" she asked, stowing her weapon and almost flattening herself on the board for speed.

If Chisnall was killed or incapacitated, she would be in charge. Was that the reason for the pain in the pit of her stomach?

"Monster! Talk to me!" she said.

"Just got here," Monster said in her ear. "Chisnall looks . . . okay."

A gasping sound on the comm sounded suspiciously like Chisnall, but Price forced herself to ignore it, to believe the words Monster had spoken, to continue barreling down into the murk of the tunnel.

Kriz leaned into a sharp corner, then saw that two railway lines now crossed directly in front of her. She jumped, bouncing the board over the rail, landing easily on the other side with a short laugh. *Try and match that!*

In the same instant she realized her mistake.

The railway line ran right alongside the command center, but a sheer rock wall blocked any access. She might be able to climb the wall, but not before her pursuer would be on her.

Kriz elected to stay on the tracks, heading away from the command center. Here the tracks were a twisted tangle of metal rails, at least eight merging lines, crisscrossing like a child's play set. Every cross meant a metal bar across the path and she grinned, confident of her returning skills. She hopped and leaped from track to track, sometimes running on concrete, sometimes on gravel, each time landing squarely on all wheels, with her balance intact. Surely nobody would be able to match such skill. *Even the great Tzukich, the world champion T-boarder, would have been proud of such moves.*

Behind her she saw her pursuer jump a track, then another, then fall after a sideways skip across a rail, losing valuable time.

Kriz skipped across another of the heavy rusted metal rails and landed square.

Perfect!

A rising slope took her to a bridge where a flimsy chain-link fence separated the railway line from a small parking lot.

She glanced back again. Her pursuer was well behind, getting up after another fall. She had time. Kriz jumped off the T-board, threw it over the fence, and climbed over. Gunning the T-board once more, she took a road that she knew looped right back to the command center. She took the curve at maximum speed, leaning low, fingertips brushing on the ground. The road straightened, only a short stretch now to the command center. And safety.

Kriz didn't see the runaway T-board until it was almost on her and by then it was far too late. She tried to veer out of its way, but that made matters worse—she was off balance when it hit her broadside.

Tumbling sideways, she hit the rough asphalt at speed, gathering grazes and scrapes as she came to a halt, in time to see the dark figure in the side street raising a coil-gun at her. She felt a kick in her chest and gasped air back into her lungs, knowing even as she did that it was the wrong thing to do. With the air came the acrid taste of powder, but that only lasted for a brief, terrible moment before the blackness rose up like a sheet and covered her.

▪ ▪ ▪

Price skidded to a halt alongside Barnard, who was dragging the Bzadian into a small park, concealing her in a stand of bushy shrubs.

"Where were you?" Price asked. "Where's the Tsar?"

"We couldn't get to the end of the bridge in time. There were security fences. She climbed them. I figured out where she was going and cut her off here."

"You figured out where she was going. How?"

"She recognized Chisnall just before she shot him. That meant it had to be the Coastal Defense officer he spoke to on the video screen on the island. Their command center is at the old Victoria Barracks, so I figured that was where she was going and beat her to it."

"That was smart," Price said.

"Try not to sound so surprised," Barnard said.

The Tsar arrived, skidding around a corner on two wheels. Price stared at Barnard for a moment, then shook her head and spoke into her comm. "We got her." She stilled her breathing and asked calmly, matter-of-factly, "How is Ryan?"

"Oscar Kilo. Will be fine," Monster said.

"No, seriously, how is he?" Price asked.

"Seriously, he fine. The first bullet messed up the armor. Second bullet is doing the damage. It crack a rib. Nothing more."

"He's really Oscar Kilo?" Price asked, daring to hope a little.

"He going to be fine. Seriously," Monster said.

"Thank God," Price said.

"Thank Monster," Barnard said.

Wilton said, "That's what happens when you take on real bullets with popguns."

12. THE RACE FOR AMBERLEY

[0540 hours local time]
[Ipswich, New Bzadia]

CHISNALL WINCED AT THE SHARP PAIN IN HIS CHEST. HE eased forward a little, pushing aside a branch, giving himself a clearer, wider view out of the small group of young trees he was concealed in. There had been no movement in his sector since they had arrived and set up a secure perimeter, but he wasn't taking any chances.

They were in the small city of Ipswich, inland from Brisbane. The first major destination of the task force. It was here that the fleet of MPCs, tanks, and artillery would emerge from the river to continue the next stage of the journey, Amberley Air Base.

The others were lying or crouching among bushes, but he was standing. Lying would put pressure on his chest, and the way he was feeling now, he would probably black out. Chisnall adjusted his new body armor, trying to get comfortable, but no matter what he did, the heavy material weighed on his aching ribs.

He was lucky to have the armor. One of the first few MPCs to emerge from the river had been a supply vehicle.

Chisnall zoomed his NV goggles on the trees at the end of the road to check out some movement. Nothing. Just leaves muttering idly in an early-morning breeze.

The scent of the river—a pungent, musty smell—was strong here. Recent rain made the ground soft. A column of ants, the nightshift from a nearby nest, was marching in single file across the edge of the sidewalk. Like soldiers, he thought. And their existence was almost as precarious. He could wipe out the entire column with a single footstep.

The clandestine part of the mission was nearly over. There was no way to conceal the emergence of the task force from the river, particularly in the orange-gray early-morning light.

The rest of the Angel Team was spread out to his right. Like him, in concealment, watching, wary, every sense alert for anyone, anything, that could compromise the operation at this most delicate stage.

The Demons were to his left. He could hear shuffling and the occasional murmur or laugh as they talked among themselves. His own team was quieter and better disciplined.

The two teams were arrayed around a park on the south side of the river. On the north side, where there was little danger of detection, the operation was taking place in the lee of a huge shopping mall that was silent and empty at this time of the morning. Mission planners had assured him it would be deserted, but even so he had tasked Wilton to keep an eye on it with his long-range NV scope in case anyone was prowling its corridors in the darkness.

Time passed. There seemed to be no progress extracting the vehicles from the river. Chisnall checked the time on his wrist computer more than once, growing increasingly conscious of the timeline they had to stick to. But there was nothing to do but wait. War was not like the movies. He had discovered that long ago. Movies were full of action and excitement. War was hours and hours of tedium punctuated by short moments of sheer terror.

He could hear a mosquito's annoying, high-pitched whine, fading in and out as the insect made circles around his head. And he wasn't the only one to be targeted. Chisnall heard a slap and Monster said, "Monster hate mosquito!"

There was laughter from the team.

"Big tough Monster, afraid of a tiny little insect?" Price said.

"I can't stand them either," Wilton said.

"They never worry me," Price said.

"They wouldn't dare," the Tsar said.

"Do you think mosquitoes bite Pukes?" Wilton asked.

"Probably," Price said. "After all, they share most of our DNA."

"I still can't figure out how the Pukes came to be so closely related to us," Wilton said. "Don't they come from a different galaxy or somewhere?"

"I told you once before, Wilton," Chisnall said. "Better minds than ours are working on that stuff."

"You know, the ancient Nazca people drew huge pictures in the desert that can only be seen from high above the Earth," the Tsar said.

"Did they race stock cars around them?" Wilton asked.

"That's NASCAR, moron," Price said.

"The pictures are so large that they could only be seen from an airplane or a spaceship," the Tsar said.

"Why? Back then they didn't have airplanes or . . ." They could just about hear the cogs spinning in Wilton's brain. "Oh, cool!"

"Or maybe they drew them for their gods," Barnard said.

"The ancient Mayans drew pictures that look a lot like astronauts," the Tsar said. "How cool is that!"

"Seriously?" Wilton asked.

"Some people think so," the Tsar said.

"And some people don't," Barnard said.

"So it's probably a coincidence, then, that the Mayans predicted the end of the world in 2012," the Tsar said. "That's when the Pukes started arriving."

"I thought they came in 2014," Wilton said.

"The year 2014 was when the transporters arrived," the Tsar said. "The first representatives were negotiating in secret with Earth governments from December 2012. The Mayans had it on the nail."

"They didn't predict the end of the world," Barnard said. "That was a misunderstanding of their writings."

"They sure as hell predicted something in 2012," the Tsar said.

"Wilton, how's that mall?" Chisnall asked, trying to keep them focused. It had been a long night, but their concentration was as important as ever.

"If you're planning on a little shopping, you're all out of luck," Wilton said. "Ain't nobody home."

"Keep an eye on it," Chisnall said.

In the Mater Hospital, on the south bank of the Brisbane River, Major Zara Kriz woke up. It was not a sudden awakening but rather a gradual shift from a gray world of indeterminate shapes to clearly defined faces and the white walls of a hospital room.

Something tremendously important was troubling her, but she could not remember what it was.

"Hello, I am Huzfa." The voice came from a doctor who was leaning over her, examining her eyes with a bright light that hurt like a knife. Kriz blinked and turned her head away.

"And you are?"

"Kriz, Major Zara Kriz," she managed.

"Do you know where you are?" Huzfa asked.

Two nurses were moving around her, doing things, although she had no idea what. Tubes ran into her arms from a machine by the bed.

"Hospital," Kriz croaked.

"Do you know why?" Huzfa asked.

Kriz shook her head.

"Some kind of narcotic," Huzfa said. "We found residue of it on your clothing."

Narcotic. That made no sense. Why would there have been a narcotic on her clothes?

"You also have severe bruising on your chest and back," Huzfa said.

Even through the haze, the painful kick of the bullets was a vivid memory. She should be dead. She had not been wearing armor. Or was that just a hallucination?

"You were lucky," Huzfa said. "You were found in a park, and we were able to counteract most of the effects of the drug."

There was a disapproving tone in his voice as if he thought Kriz had somehow done this to herself.

"Which park?" Kriz asked.

Huzfa shook his head. "I don't know the name of it. Not far from here. Down by the river."

The river! Images of great metal river monsters flashed through her head, and it all came flooding back.

"What time is it?" Kriz asked.

Huzfa pointed to a clock on the wall. "You were unconscious nearly five hours."

"Get me a phone," Kriz said, and the croakiness in her voice was gone.

"You need to rest—" Huzfa began, but Kriz cut him off.

"Get me a phone," she said, and outlined several very unpleasant things that would happen to him if he didn't obey.

"While we're waiting, everybody renourish and rehydrate," Chisnall said.

"Breakfast!" Monster said.

"I don't know how you can eat in the middle of all this," Barnard said.

"Is most important meal of day," Monster said.

"Might be your last meal—better make it count," Price said.

"Nice. Now I'm not hungry either," the Tsar said.

"You're no use to me if you die of starvation," Chisnall said.

"And I thought it was new weapons and better tactics that were going to win this war," the Tsar said. "Turns out it's cornflakes and tinned fruit."

"Be happy it's not Puke food," Price said. "Green sludge in a toothpaste tube. Once we break off from the main task force, that's all we'll be allowed to eat."

"And they're all vegetarians!" Wilton said.

"What's wrong with that?" Barnard said. "The Pukes don't believe in going around slaughtering and eating the other inhabitants of their planet."

"Except us," Price said.

"They don't eat us," Barnard said.

"Not yet," Wilton said.

"What's the difference between eating beef and eating broccoli?" the Tsar asked. "They're both living creatures when you think about it."

"Cows don't want to die," Barnard said. "Broccoli doesn't care."

"How do you know that broccoli doesn't care?" Wilton asked.

"Cow taste good," Monster said, licking his lips.

Soft footsteps came from behind Chisnall and he looked around as two German Kommandos Spezialkrafte approached, dark and dangerous in their black uniforms. More of the Kommandos appeared from the riverbank.

"Anything?" one of the Kommandos asked. He was a tough-looking captain, about thirty years old and unshaven.

"Dead quiet so far," Chisnall said.

"Okay, thanks."

"What's going on at the river?" Chisnall asked.

"Problems with the ramps," the Kommando captain said. "The rain has softened the banks of the river. The engineers have managed to rig something, but it is slow work."

The Kommando captain set about deploying his squad, in much the same locations as the Angels and Demons had been using.

"We've been relieved," Chisnall said on the comm. "Meet me by the railway tracks."

Chisnall heard a quiet conversation between Barnard and the Kommando captain, in German, but he could not understand what was said. They seemed to know each other. The discussion was brief and somber.

The captain moved on and Chisnall motioned to his team to gather around.

"From here on the mission is very"—he stopped, searching for the right word—"delicate."

"We can handle delicate," the Tsar said.

"This from the master of subtlety," Barnard said.

The Tsar grinned and poked his tongue out at her.

"Stay focused," Chisnall said. "We've made it this far. Now we need to get to the air base without attracting attention and provide recon until the task force is ready to attack. But they're running behind schedule, and if anything alerts Amberley Air Base before the task force gets out of the river, then this is going to be a slaughterhouse. Everybody ready?"

"I was born ready," the Tsar said.

Barnard stuck two fingers near her mouth and pretended to vomit.

"We're good to go, LT," Price said.

Chisnall checked the time on his wrist computer. It was nearly 06:00 hours and the sun was well awake.

He stood carefully, trying not to put any pressure on his cracked rib, but despite his efforts, it screamed with pain, and he had to stand still for a moment to clear the swarm of black dots that were circling before his eyes. The others had already moved off, except for Barnard, who was standing beside him, watching him.

"You all right, LT?" she asked.

"I'm okay," he said.

He switched off his comm while he steadied himself. "What was that about? With the German guy."

"The Kommando? Nothing."

"What did he have to say? Something about the mission?"

"No, he just asked if I was okay," Barnard said.

"Do you know him?" Chisnall asked.

"Not really," Barnard said. "I met him briefly on the voyage out."

Chisnall wondered if it would be prying to ask more. He didn't get the chance, as Varmint, followed by the rest of the Demon Team, appeared out of the trees.

Varmint got a half smile from Barnard, Chisnall noted. A simple acknowledgment that seemed to conceal something deeper, something unsaid.

They had spent a week on board the HMS *Amazon* before transferring to the submarine for the last part of the trip. Enough time for Barnard to meet the Kommando. Still, Chisnall couldn't help the feeling that he wasn't getting the full story.

Price said she thought Barnard could be trusted. But they had all been fooled before.

He started walking, and despite each step jarring his rib, there was no return of the dizziness.

The Angels were waiting on the other side of the railway tracks. Price was clearly angry with Monster about something, although with the comm off, Chisnall couldn't tell what it was.

"I don't know what's up between those two," he said as they walked, not sure why he was confiding in Barnard. Maybe it was the painkillers, or maybe he was coming to respect her insight and her rather brutal honesty. "They got on fine at Uluru, but now they can't stand each other."

"Jeez, Ryan, is that what you think?" Barnard said. "And you're a leader of men?"

Chisnall stopped briefly and looked at her. "What do you mean?"

Barnard kept walking. "You figure it out."

Although there was plenty of room, the Demons crossed

the railway line right where the Angels were standing, pushing their way through the assembled group—except for Monster, who was given a wide berth.

"Watch where you're going, buttwipe," Price said.

"Aren't they cute when they're angry?" Miscreant said.

"Go to hell," Wilton said.

"We can't. We got kicked out," Hooligan said, and turned to Yobbo for a high five.

"Failed the IQ test, probably," Price said. "Even hell has standards."

"Obviously Team Angel doesn't," Miscreant said.

"What are you still doing here?" Chisnall asked.

Varmint shrugged. "Our MPC with all the demolition charges is stuck somewhere back in that river. You Angels want to fly over there and lift it out for us, we'll be on our way."

"Hey, how many Angels does it take to change a lightbulb?" Miscreant asked.

"None," Yobbo said. "They just watch someone else do it."

"Yeah, and how many Demons does it take to change a lightbulb?" Wilton asked.

"Only one," the Tsar said, counting with his middle finger.

"Nope, none," Miscreant said. "Demons aren't afraid of the dark."

13. ULURU

[0600 hours local time]
[Uluru Military Base, New Bzadia]

THE INCOMING CALL INTERRUPTED THE PEACE OF THE ROOM.

The communications and control room at Uluru was a large dome, featureless except for the video screens that ringed the room at head height. Twenty-six circular desks were scattered across the floor of the dome in a pattern, which although seemingly random, was optimized for maximum efficiency when all the desks were occupied. That would only be in the event of a major alert or incident, however, and currently only three of the desks had operators at them, all of whom looked bored.

It was nearly shift change, and it had been a long, uneventful night, like all nights. At least, since *that night.*

There were four staff on duty altogether. The fourth was the shift commander, sitting at his desk on a raised circular platform in the center of the room.

He had one leg propped on a second chair, although that did little to relieve the aching. Most of the bones in his body had been shattered when the humans had attacked Uluru, but that leg had been the worst.

The incoming call lit up screens all around the room. While probably nothing, it was at least an interruption of the monotony.

All three of the operators reached for the call, but the young female, Ibazu, was quickest.

The shift commander could see her face from his vantage point and tried to gauge from her expression whether it was anything to warrant him shifting his leg from where it rested.

Confusion was what he saw, rather than alarm.

He sent a message to Ibazu's console. *Put it up.*

She glanced up at him, spoke briefly to the caller for a few more seconds, then punched the call up onto the loudspeakers.

"I am Lieutenant Yozi Gonzale," the shift commander said.

A female voice, thick, barely more than a mumble, responded. "I am Major Zara Kriz," she said, and began to talk. Yozi listened, and as he did, his still-healing leg came down off the chair. He leaned forward at his desk, the pain forgotten.

Even while Kriz was groggily spouting nonsense about river monsters and scumbugz, he was sending another message to Ibazu's console.

Contact the regional patrol base. I want a scan of the river immediately.

Ibazu picked up her phone.

The patrol base was located at the old Brisbane Airport at the mouth of the river. A sweep of the river, from the base, along to Ipswich would take the rotorcraft approximately fifteen minutes.

The race for Amberley had begun.

The Angels moved softly through a waking city, avoiding anyone they could and casually greeting anyone they could not avoid.

One elderly Bzadian, agitated at the sight of armed troops in his quiet suburban street, came out of his house and protested. Chisnall and Monster took him back inside and, after checking the house for other residents, gave him a shot of Puke spray. Rheumy eyes filled with spite followed them as they locked the front door and left.

They were well out in the suburbs now. Little houses on individual plots lined up in neat rows on neat streets. To the human eye, the yards of the houses were unkempt and overgrown. Lawns were not mowed, hedges were untrimmed, and some houses seemed on the verge of being overrun by the greenery around them. That was the Bzadian way, Chisnall knew. They lived more in harmony with the natural world than humans did, and felt less need to cut, slash, tidy and prettify the living things around them.

He kept one ear on the task force radio channel. It was

distracting, listening to all the comms chatter, but he wanted to know about their progress.

He checked their own position. They were almost at Amberley. They had made good time.

One more turn took them into a dead-end street, leaving the asphalt and moving onto farmland, overgrown and wild. Their T-boards pushed through long grasses, which sprang back behind them. A couple of fences blocked their way, but they were for cattle and easily climbed over. The team entered a small forest and stopped just inside the far edge, looking down from a slight rise to the flat plain beyond, where the buildings of Amberley Air Base sat silent, a sleeping giant they did not want to wake.

Two runways created a huge cross that pointed to the south. At the northern end, large hangars rose up against the early-morning light.

Lining the runway to the north were row after row of fast movers. There were at least fifty or sixty Type Ones, the small nimble jets that were so dangerous to human aircraft. In neat diagonal rows behind those were the Type Twos, air-to-ground attack craft, and on two flat tarmac areas to the north of that were the Dragons, the huge, formidable castles of the air, bristling with armaments and almost invulnerable to attack.

A few Bzadians were moving around the airfield, and a security patrol in a Land Rover was following the perimeter fence line, but it was otherwise quiet.

"Task Force Actual, this is Angel One," Chisnall said.

"Task Force Actual, clear copy," came the reply.

"We have eyes on Target Bravo, all clear, all quiet," Chisnall said.

"Solid copy, Angel One. We are waiting for a rotorcraft to pass by. Might be heading to the air base. Make sure you stay out of sight."

"Solid copy, Task Force Actual. We'll sit nice and tight."

They kept good cover behind the trees and waited.

"Big Dog," the Tsar said a few moments later. "Got that slow mover on the scope. Looks like it's coming right this way."

"ETA?" Chisnall asked.

"About four minutes."

"I've got a bad feeling about this," Wilton said.

So did Chisnall, but he was careful not to share it.

Kriz made it back to the Coastal Defense Command Center in time to see the rotorcraft arrive at Ipswich.

It was only a few minutes' drive from the hospital, and the ambulance that took her must have broken some kind of record, lights flashing and siren screaming despite the fact that the roads were almost deserted.

If she woke up a few residents, tough.

The ambulance attendant went with her into the command center, holding her arm. She was grateful, because otherwise she would have fallen.

As she sank into her chair, the screens were already full of the images from the high-resolution night-vision camera mounted on the underside of the patrol craft.

"Anything?" she asked.

Nanzi, who had been manning Kriz's desk, shook his head. "It's been completely clear," he said.

"What about the mist on the river?" Kriz asked.

"Gradually clearing," Nanzi said. "But thermal imaging has been clear also."

"Who's the captain of that rotorcraft?" Kriz asked.

"Lieutenant Zzaker," Nanzi said, referring to a screen.

"Get her on the line now," Kriz said.

The voice came through her headset within a few seconds.

"Where are you now?" Kriz demanded, with no time for formalities.

"We're on the Bremer River," Zzaker said. She was young, judging by her voice. "Over North Ipswich, just following the curve of the river around to the mall."

"Still all clear?" Kriz asked, although she could see on the screens that it was.

"Yes, so far and . . . Wait a second."

Kriz found her attention drawn to the speaker box on the wall, not the video screen.

"There may be some kind of activity up ahead, opposite the mall," Zzaker said. "Just coming into range now. There's something in the river too. I'm going in for a closer look."

"No!" Kriz yelled, but she was far too late.

The video feed came into focus: the soldiers scurrying around on the shore; the vehicles starting to line up in the adjacent parking lot; the long line of vehicles still semisubmerged in the river.

"Full alert!" Kriz yelled at Nanzi. To the speaker on the wall she shouted, "Get out of there!"

A bright star blossomed in the middle of the video screen, growing larger and larger.

Zzaker's voice on the radio, no longer directed at Kriz: "Incoming! Countermeasures! Evasive maneuvers."

The image on the screen swung wildly as the gimbal-mounted cameras struggled to cope with the violent movements of the aircraft. The bright dot grew, drawing a fiery pattern in the middle of the screen. It filled the screen just before it all went blank.

Half a second later they heard the thunderclap of sound, rattling the windows of the command center.

"Who do I call?" Nanzi cried.

"Everyone," Kriz said distantly.

14. STEEL ON TARGET

[0620 hours local time]

[Amberley Air Base, New Bzadia]

"THIS VERY NOT GOOD," MONSTER SAID.

They were still on the eastern slope of the small wooded hill, on the ridgeline, with a clear view of the huge Amberley Air Base slumbering away below them.

But now, the awakening of the air base was as dramatic as it was sudden.

Floodlights blared into life. The runways became great glowing strips. The hangar doors began to open. At the barracks, transportation vehicles were starting up, ready to bring pilots and ground crews to the waiting rows of jets and rotorcraft.

Chisnall felt bile rise into his throat as he realized what that meant for the men and women of the task force, stuck back at the river.

"Angel One to Task Force Actual," Chisnall said. "Major activity at Target Bravo. I repeat, major activity at Target Bravo."

"Solid copy, Angel One." It was Colonel Fairbrother, the task force commander. A gray-haired marine, about fifty years old, he had served in the British Army until its remains had been absorbed into the US Army and Marine Corps. Regarded by some as a brilliant commander and by others (mostly Americans) as an eccentric, he was renowned for wearing a sword into battle. Actually, it was a cavalry sabre, and it was not merely ceremonial. According to legend, he had used it on more than one occasion.

Fairbrother said, "We knew this would happen sooner or later. Now let's get those bloody vehicles out of that bloody river before the entire bloody Bzadian air force gets here."

"There's no time," Price said, her eyes fixed on the airfield. "Those first fast movers will be off the ground within five mikes."

"Task Force Actual, anticipate enemy aerial activity, your sector, five mikes," Chisnall said.

"Five mikes! Angel One, we need more time. Is there anything you can do?"

"We'll try, sir," Chisnall said, without any idea of what his team could do against the power and size of the forces arrayed below.

Security forces were scrambling to protect the perimeter of the air base. Prepared defensive positions and gun towers were coming to life as Bzadian soldiers, some still pulling on their uniforms, hurried into place.

A low growl came from the engines of the Type Ones in the first row. The engines auto-started to warm up before takeoff.

"Angel One to Task Force Actual, we have prestart initiation on Type Ones," Chisnall said.

"Solid copy, Angel One." It was the comm officer's voice that came back to him.

"We have to get down there and do something," Price said. "Or this operation is over right now."

"Do what?" Chisnall asked. "We'd never even breach the perimeter."

"Even if we could take out the defenses and get past the security fence, we'd be taking on jets with puffer rounds," Wilton said.

"If we don't do something, you can wave the operation bye-bye," the Tsar said.

"What are you suggesting? The Charge of the Light Brigade?" Chisnall said. "It's suicide."

"It's suicide either way," the Tsar said. "At least we go out fighting!"

"Are the guns emplaced yet?" Barnard asked.

"The what?" Price asked.

"The artillery. The light-guns. Are they emplaced yet?"

Chisnall caught her drift. "Task Force Actual, this is Angel One."

"Not now, Angel One, we're busy."

"Urgent break-in, Task Force Actual, highest priority."

"Go ahead, Angel One."

"Are the light-guns emplaced yet?"

There was a brief pause while she checked. She came back quickly. "Emplaced and finishing calibration, but the FFC is still here."

The FFC was the forward fire control, without which the artillery was pretty much shooting blind. Usually a forward observation post would feed information back to the artillery battery about where the rounds were falling, enabling them to adjust fire.

"Task Force Actual, suggest begin bombardment immediately," Chisnall said. "We will provide forward fire control."

There was a brief silence on the radio while discussion took place at the other end; then Fairbrother again picked up the microphone. "They'll start firing within a few seconds. You call it in. Make 'em count, Angel One. You're all we've got."

"Take out the center of the cross," Barnard said, pointing to where the two runways crossed each other. "The Pukes use multiple runways for fast takeoffs. But if we can take out the cross, it'll knock both runways out at once."

A roll of thunder came from behind them. The first artillery shells were already screaming over their heads.

Chisnall switched to the fire support channel.

"Artillery Support, this is Angel One."

"Solid copy, Angel One, firing for range and angle, will adjust on your say. You call the shots."

The screaming sound turned into a whistling roar, and the high-explosive rounds landed in a tight bracket on the perimeter fence line, dirt and concrete erupting into the air, destroying one of the guard towers but leaving the runways untouched.

Chisnall hesitated, trying to estimate distances and angles. They trained for this, but it was the first time he had ever used it in the field.

"Let me do it, LT," Barnard said.

"I've got it," Chisnall said.

"Call the shots, Angel One," the artilleryman said in his ear. "Call the shots."

"LT, I can do this," Barnard said.

"I got this!"

Another round of shells whistled overhead, landing in almost the same place as the first.

"Fifty and a ton, LT!" Barnard yelled over of the roar of the explosions. "Tell them, LT!"

"Adjust forward fifty meters, left a hundred meters," Chisnall said.

In the distance behind them, artillery thundered again, followed by the screaming shells overhead. This time the impact was almost on target, landing in an empty field next to the apex of the crossed runways.

At the northern and western ends of the runway, the first two fast movers had lined up for takeoff. The first began to accelerate with the roar of engines and tongues of fire from the afterburners. After a few seconds, the jet on the western runway did the same. Already a third jet was lining up on the northern runway.

"Adjust forward ten, right twenty!" Chisnall yelled. "Fire for effect. Now, now, now!"

The Bzadian jets were streaking forward, a few seconds apart. The first was nose up, ready to lift off. Behind them, the next jets were starting to move. Chisnall had only once before seen the precision of the Bzadian air force in action, two lines of jets lifting off the deck almost as one, fitting together as closely as a zipper.

But the next round of shells was already falling. The edge of the runway exploded, right in the middle of the cross, dirt and tarmac spewing into the air beside the wingtip of the leftmost of the fast movers. The shock wave lifted the wing of the jet, the other wing smashing into the ground, and the whole craft cartwheeled, a tangled fiery mess of steel and burning fuel spinning uncontrollably into a neat row of rotorcraft parked near the runway, scattering them like bowling pins. More explosions came as the rotorcraft burst into flames, the effect rippling out through the massed ranks as craft after craft exploded. The second jet, on the western runway, tried to lift up to avoid the craters that had suddenly appeared, but it didn't have enough wing speed. It hopped up into the air for a few meters, but then the back wheels crashed down and clipped the edge of one of the craters, the jet breaking in two as it slammed into the runway in a ball of fire.

The next two planes, already committed to the takeoff, added to the inferno, now completely blocking both runways. The following jets cut back their engines, with nowhere to go.

"Right on target. Commence spread, right fifty meters," Chisnall said.

Thunder and lightning from behind them and the runway began to dance as a series of explosions rippled down the centerline.

"Expect company," the Tsar said.

Chisnall switched his gaze to the perimeter. Gates had opened and a stream of soldiers was emerging at speed, scattering around the surrounding area in teams of four.

"They know there's a forward fire control somewhere," Chisnall said.

"They don't know where," the Tsar said.

"Not yet," Wilton muttered.

"LT, I can take over the FFC," Barnard said. "It's going to get real busy here real quick."

"It's okay, Barnard," Chisnall said. "I got it covered."

"Keep doing what you're doing, LT. We'll worry about the soldiers," Price said, her coil-gun springing into her arms. She rested on the earth mound that was the top of the ridge and took careful aim. "Nobody fires until I do. We're not going to give away our position until we know they've definitely located us."

"Adjust fifty left, forward one hundred," Chisnall said, focusing only on the air base below him.

The immediate danger from the fast movers was gone. The jets couldn't take off on a runway that was now a shredded wasteland of flaming metal, broken tarmac, and piles of dirt. He walked the artillery onto a field full of rotorcraft that was buzzing, building up blade speed for liftoff.

"Right on target," Chisnall said as the first shells fell in the center of the field. "Use as center, radial spread eighty meters."

The field filled with smoke and flames, and the air shuddered with the scream of tortured metal as rotor blades fractured and disintegrated. Rotorcraft leaped and spun out of control as the shells exploded around them, while others simply disintegrated under direct hits. Fire spread. Ammunition on the gunships exploded throughout the field.

Incredibly, two rotorcraft managed to lift off amid the maelstrom, rising above the airfield, front edges dipping as they raced to attack the river.

"Azoh!" Wilton said, but even as he said it, one of the rotorcraft exploded in midair, a sudden bright star surrounded by crumpled metal and fiery streaks of burning fuel. The shock wave swept over the Angels, sucking the breath out of Chisnall's lungs as he realized what had happened. It was a lucky shot. A one in a million. The rotorcraft had run into one of the incoming artillery shells.

The other rotorcraft did not last much longer.

It swept over the Angels' heads, not seeing them, or not caring, heading for the river.

It never made it that far.

Thunder sounded above them and Chisnall saw the rotorcraft, out of control, spinning rapidly to the earth, the victim of another javelin missile.

"Get down!"

Something thudded into him, knocking him to the ground.

He tried, and failed, not to scream at the stabbing pain from his ribs. Monster was lying on top of him and Chisnall started to ask him what he thought he was doing when the tree trunks above them began to split and splinter.

The hammering of coil-guns told him that their hiding place was no longer a secret.

"Keep calling the shots," Price said as the Angel Team returned fire. "We've got it covered."

Several of the Bzadian soldiers dropped, but the other squads were converging on their position, maintaining a constant barrage that kept the Angels' heads down as they approached. The effect on the surrounding trees was like someone taking to them with a chainsaw. Leaves and small branches danced and shattered; larger branches and tree trunks spat sawdust. Dirt jumped up into their faces.

The Bzadians advanced, closing in from eighty meters, seventy meters. It was all Chisnall could do to risk the occasional glance to try and direct the artillery fire where it was most needed.

Sixty meters. He would have to bring the artillery down on the advancing troops if they were to have any chance at all.

"New coordinates," Chisnall shouted into the radio over the wall of sound that was the battle. "Immediate effect." He got the coordinates of their own position from his wrist computer and mentally added fifty meters. "Fire for range and accuracy. Danger close."

"Danger close" let the artillery know that they were firing in the vicinity of friendly troops. There was a brief pause while the artillery team adjusted their guns, then the familiar thunder. This time, though, the sound was different. It wasn't the scream of shells passing high overhead, but rather the rising whistle of shells falling close to their position. Too close.

"Incoming!" Price screamed.

Alizza was strapping on his coil-gun when Yozi rounded the corner into their ready room. Yozi didn't limp, but it took a concerted effort. Alizza looked up in surprise to see him.

"Save me a place, old friend," Yozi said.

"When did you get back on active duty?" Alizza asked.

"Just now," Yozi said.

"Who authorized it?"

"I did."

Alizza grinned. "It is definitely scumbugz?"

"It is," Yozi said. "They've infiltrated via the Brisbane River. Seems like the target is the Amberley Air Base."

"The last time scumbugz came here I fear we let them off too lightly," Alizza said.

"That won't happen again," Yozi said, and began to kit up.

Chisnall curled into a ball and covered his ears with his hands as high explosive shells slammed into the forest around them.

The explosions were mainly tree bursts—shells hitting tree trunks and exploding, shattering the trunks and sending meter-long splinters of wood flying throughout the forest. One embedded itself in the ground a foot away from Chisnall, who stared at it, stunned, his ears ringing from the explosions.

"Adjust fire, adjust fire!" he yelled.

"Forward fifty meters," he managed to get out just before another barrage of shells pulverized trees around their position.

Bzadian troops, taking advantage of the lack of firing from the tree line, were running across open ground toward the Angels.

The next artillery barrage fell right among them. The earth shook and shivered as more and more shells came screaming in, and those Bzadians that still could ran for their lives. The open field had become a killing ground.

"LT," Wilton said. "Fast movers!"

Back at the airfield, a row of Type Twos had lined up on a long grass strip beside the runway.

"Get the artillery on it, now!" the Tsar yelled.

"If you do that, the Pukes'll be all over us!" Price yelled back.

"If you don't, those Type Twos are going to rip the task force to shreds!" the Tsar said.

"If we're dead, then who's going to call the shots for the artillery anyway?" Price said.

"It's your call, LT," Barnard said.

It was an impossible choice.

"Revert to original coordinates," Chisnall said on the radio. "Adjust fire back ten meters. Fire for effect."

Explosions ripped up the dirt of the grassy field. A Type Two, in the middle of takeoff, tried to avoid a huge pothole that had suddenly erupted. Its nose dropped into the ground, ripping off, and the jet slid across the grass before coming to a halt in the middle of the field.

With the shifting of the artillery barrage, the Bzadian troops were already on their way back up the hillside toward the Angels' position. Their faces were covered, and as they closed, Chisnall realized they had replaced their visors with gas masks. They had adapted quickly to the puffer ammunition.

"Rotorcraft, far end of the field," Barnard said.

Chisnall could see several rotorcraft already lifting off at the rear of the air base. "Immediate adjustment, forward one hundred, right sixty," he said, estimating the distances by eye. "Air burst, I repeat, air burst."

The next round of shells exploded in midair, above the rising rotorcraft, shattering cockpits and rotor blades. In twos and threes the Bzadian craft plummeted to the ground. But already more were lifting off from other locations around the air base.

Somehow, Chisnall found himself removed from the battle, operating on a higher plane where all that mattered were coordinates and numbers. The air base took on a kind of virtual reality in his head. He threw shells with the power of his thoughts, hurling lightning bolts at the enemy craft, barely conscious of the numbers that his dry lips were streaming back to the artillery base.

Only when the dirt in front of his eyes exploded with the impact of bullets, momentarily blinding him, did his attention come back to the advancing Bzadian soldiers, crawling across the open fields below. He switched to the task force channel and said, "Task Force Actual, this is Angel One. Request immediate ground support. We are in danger of being overrun."

"Forward units are heading your way, Angel Team. Sit tight. They'll be with you in five mikes."

"Task Force Actual, we don't have five mikes," Chisnall said.

The Bzadian soldiers were advancing steadily across the open ground, firing as they came, their bullets becoming more accurate with every meter. They staggered under the impact of the Angels' puffer rounds but kept coming.

More firing now, much closer, but it took Chisnall a few seconds to comprehend where it was coming from. It wasn't until a thump on the back of his body armor knocked him forward that he realized the firing was behind them.

"LT!" Price yelled out.

He pushed himself up and twisted around to glimpse a Bzadian uniform coming up through the trees behind them. In the confusion, smoke, and shelling, a squad of Bzadians had circled around, flanking them. It was an obvious tactic and he should have been prepared for it. It was what he would have done in their position. But his concentration had been on calling the shots for the artillery. Now they were sandwiched between two groups of Bzadians and completely exposed at the rear.

It was surrender or die. There was no other choice.

"Keep calling the shots, LT," Monster said in a low voice, unleashing a stream of bullets into the trees behind them. The puffers were exploding off the trees in such numbers that a gray cloud was forming in the forest, but it was of no use against the gas-masked Bzadians.

A shot cracked off the side of his helmet, dazing him. Bullets were all around them as the Bzadians opened up at close range.

"Put your weapons down!" he yelled to his team. They had no chance of survival. Their only hope was to surrender.

"No puking way!" the Tsar yelled.

"Death to Azoh!" Wilton yelled.

"See you in the next life!" The Tsar kept firing. A shot from the forest hit Chisnall on the shoulder, spinning him around, facedown into the dirt. His broken rib screamed fire, and another round smashed the armor on his right arm. One more shot and that was it. He was a dead man.

He tried to lift his gun, to return fire, but couldn't. He waited for the bullet that would pierce his ruined armor and end his life. It didn't come. The firing from the woods behind them had stopped.

"Friendlies coming out," came a voice that he knew well. "Are y'all okay?"

"Angels, hold your fire," Chisnall said as someone emerged from the trees through the swirling smoke and puffer clouds. It was Varmint, a can of Puke spray in a clenched hand, a Bzadian gas mask in the other.

"Angel Team, status check," Chisnall said, and unbelievably got a chorus of "Oscar Kilo."

Varmint said, "Call the shots so we can get the hell out of here."

The Demon Team was unloading their coil-guns and slotting in new ammunition cartridges. Bzadian ammunition,

Chisnall realized. They had done what they said they would, swapped puffers for hard bullets, taking them from the soldiers.

The Demons spread out, dropping to the ground and crawling to the top of the rise. From there they began to pour fire, real bullets, down on the approaching troops.

Varmint tossed Chisnall a cartridge and without hesitation he swapped it for his puffers. He heard the guns of the other Angels combine with those of the Demons, and below them the oncoming Bzadian troops broke ranks and ran under the hail of fire.

On the air base, a huge Dragon jet had somehow found a clear stretch of grass long enough to take off.

"Artillery support," Chisnall said. "New coordinates."

15. ARMOR

[0710 hours local time]
[Bzadian Coastal Defense Command, Brisbane, New Bzadia]

"WE'VE LOST AMBERLEY," NANZI SAID. "ALL COMMUNI-cations just dropped out. Last reports were of tanks attacking the perimeter."

"Any word back from the other air bases?" Kriz asked. She had to struggle not to rub at the new skin on her arm. Last time the humans had attacked, she had ended up in the hospital for months. Now they were back. She felt nauseous and took a few quick deep breaths, which seemed to help.

There were three other bases still at full strength, in north, south, and west New Bzadia.

"They're on full alert," Nanzi said, "but none of them have committed any planes yet."

"What!"

"All are reporting enemy radar contacts," Nanzi said. "They are refusing to release any aircraft. I guess they don't want to be the next Uluru."

"Or the next Amberley," Kriz said. "How far away is the general?" Until he got here, every decision was up to her.

"Ten minutes."

"What are they up to?" Kriz said.

"You don't think Amberley is their primary objective?"

"It doesn't make sense," Kriz said. "There's no strategic advantage."

"It's the biggest military target in the area," Nanzi said. "Maybe they think that by striking us here, we will have to withdraw forces from the Chukchi Peninsula to defend ourselves."

A map of the region was displayed on the big screen that covered one wall of the command center. Amberley and the army base at Enoggera were highlighted in red, along with a number of smaller military installations.

"They've gone to too much trouble," Kriz said. "They must be after something more than that."

"Like what?" Nanzi asked

"It has to be Lowood," Kriz said, zooming the map into that area. "The fuel plant. There's nothing else within a hundred kilometers."

"Azoh!" Nanzi said.

"Alert the defense commander at Borallon. See if they can intercept the scumbugz before they get anywhere near Lowood, and tell those air bases we need air support now! What's happening at Uluru?"

"Ready reaction force is already lifting off."

"Good. They're our best hope for now. How far away are they?"

"At least four hours," Nanzi said.

"What else do we have available?" Kriz asked.

Nanzi checked her computer screen. "Not much. Everything's been sent to Chukchi. Except . . ."

"What?"

"Well, they're not combat ready, but there's a full squadron of battle tanks at the Nambour factory. They've just come off the production line and are still awaiting testing."

"That's not even three hours away from Lowood." Kriz considered that. "Are the crews with them?"

"Yes. They start field tests tomorrow."

Kriz ran some quick calculations in her head. The tanks would have to be armed and equipped, and that would take at least an hour. The crews would be test personnel, not combat troops. But it was better than nothing. A lot better. "Get me the commander of that squadron," she said.

16. RESERVOIR HILL

[0715 hours local time]

[Amberley Air Base, New Bzadia]

"WHAT THE BLOODY HELL WERE YOU THINKING?" COLONEL Fairbrother asked.

Varmint stood to attention, as did Chisnall beside him. All trace of his Demon attitude was gone. For the moment at least.

"You Demons were supposed to be halfway to Wivenhoe by now," Fairbrother continued. He was seated on the other side of the command module.

From the west came a series of explosions, part of the mopping up at the air base.

"If they hadn't turned back, my team would be dead," Chisnall said.

"I wasn't addressing you, Chisnall."

"Sir, it was my decision and my mistake," Varmint said. "It won't happen again."

"Sir, the fault was mine," Chisnall said. "I was focusing on the fire control and neglected the defense of my team."

"Did I ask for your input?" Fairbrother asked.

Chisnall shook his head.

"If I had any choice, I'd court-martial you both. But right now I need you to get on with your jobs. Am I clear?"

"Clear," Varmint and Chisnall said together.

Another explosion sounded from the air base as task force troops made sure that none of the aircraft would ever fly again.

"Reservoir Hill," Fairbrother said, stabbing a finger at the map table. Another finger. "Wivenhoe Dam."

Even on the 3-D digital terrain map, Reservoir Hill didn't seem much more than a mild rise on the countryside. Wivenhoe Dam held back a huge mass of water extending to the north well beyond the bounds of the map.

"Reservoir Hill is the high ground," Fairbrother was saying. "It controls all the approaches into Lowood. Whoever holds the hill controls the town. Reservoir Hill is fortified, honeycombed with defensive positions. We would need an all-out assault to take it and we don't have time for that. That's where you come in. I need your Angels to infiltrate that hill and take out their defenses from the inside. You just have to hold it long enough for us to get in and destroy that fuel plant."

"Sir, the Pukes were wearing gas masks when they assaulted our position on the hill at Amberley," Chisnall said.

"What's your point?" Fairbrother asked.

"They figured out about our puffers," Chisnall said. "Our weapons are next to useless now. You can't expect us to take Reservoir Hill without weapons."

"Your weapons are stealth and surprise," Fairbrother said, "and Puke spray."

"But, sir—"

Fairbrother held up a hand to silence him. "See the supply sergeant on your way out. We picked up a pile of coil-gun ammo from Amberley. Tell him I gave the okay."

"What about the Demons?" Varmint asked.

"Splityard Creek," Fairbrother said, zooming the digital map. "This smaller lake and dam here, just above the main lake. It's a power facility, generating the electricity supply for the fuel plant at Lowood. Again, an all-out assault would take too much time. Your team will 'charm' your way in and take out the generators. If for any reason we don't manage to destroy the fuel plant, at least we will have cut off their power supply."

"Destroy the generators how?" Varmint asked.

"I don't care," Fairbrother said. "Just make them go away, permanently."

"Can do." Varmint grinned.

There was nothing the Demons liked better than blowing stuff up, Chisnall thought. That was what they trained for. That was what they lived for.

"What about the dam itself?" Varmint asked. "Why not blow that up? That would be more permanent."

"Wivenhoe?" Fairbrother raised his eyebrows. "Look at the size of that thing. It's a huge earthen embankment; you'd need a nuke."

Varmint shook his head. "I meant the dam here at Splityard Creek," he said.

"Even that one is pretty big," Fairbrother said. "Maybe you could, maybe you couldn't. We can't deal in maybes. Not when the existence of the human race depends on it. Your orders are to blow the generators."

"How do we get there?" Chisnall asked. "We can't roll up in one of the MPCs."

"We'll take you with us as far as the Warrego Highway," Fairbrother said. He pointed to the map again. "Aerial footage shows a few vehicles parked around these buildings, some kind of a produce market. We'll detour a little and drop you off there. Angel Team and Demon Team each appropriate one or two of the cars. Angels take the western route up to Lowood. Go fast. I need that hill out of action before we come rolling up the highway."

"And the Demons?" Varmint asked.

"You'll take the eastern route up to Wivenhoe."

"What about extraction?" Chisnall asked.

"Hervey Bay, up on the Sunshine Coast. A submarine will pick you up offshore. Full operational orders and battle maps have been sent to your wrist computer. Now get out of here."

Even as he said it, Chisnall's wrist computer vibrated with incoming data.

"Yes, sir," Chisnall said.

"Don't balls this one up, Chisnall."

"No, sir," Chisnall replied.

The Angel Team's MPC smelled of oil. It had been used to transport the ramps for the vehicles to exit the river. Bench seats folded down from the walls inside and the interior was lit with low red lighting. A lever operated the ramp, which was also the rear door. It lifted up smoothly and locked into place.

The smell reminded Chisnall of the basement garage at home. His father had owned a classic car, a 1960 Thunderbird convertible. He was always working on it.

The thought of that car made Chisnall suddenly wish he was anywhere else except here. Life had seemed so simple. The war had been a distant far-off conflict, and despite the coverage saturating the TV and online news, it hadn't seemed like something that would affect him personally.

But it didn't get much more personal than this. Here he was, right in the thick of things, again. With people who relied on him. Who depended on him to make the right decision. He shut his eyes and breathed in the oily smell, taking himself back for a moment to that garage. To the long red car with the hood up, and his father's legs sticking out from underneath.

Then he opened his eyes again, and the memory was gone. All that existed was the here and now. The danger. The mission. The team.

Their driver was a cheerful and extremely talkative PFC,

a native of Boston, judging by his accent. He grinned at them through the small metal grille that separated the driver's cab from the troop compartment.

"It's a real honor to be driving you," the driver said. "Don't mind if I say so."

"Thanks," Chisnall said, unhooking his coil-gun before taking his seat.

"I heard about what you Angels did, from one of the grunts who got out," the driver said. "We think you guys are awesome."

"Out of Uluru?" Chisnall asked, slightly confused.

"Hokkaido," the driver said.

"Of course," Chisnall said, raising an eyebrow at the Tsar. The Tsar held his gaze but did not change his expression.

"My kid brother is doing the Angel training," the driver said. "You guys got any tips for him?"

"Get out while he still can," Price said.

"Amen to that," the Tsar said, and they both laughed.

"What's his name?" Chisnall asked.

"Hayden," the driver said. "Hayden Wall."

"I'll look out for him when we get back," Chisnall said.

"*If* we get back," Barnard said.

"Don't you worry about that," the driver said. "You got the best driver in the division. I'll get you there safe and sound. That's a promise."

"Much appreciated," Chisnall said.

The engine started with a roar but the MPC didn't move. It sat idling, waiting its turn. They were the second last in line, behind the Demons and in front of an MPC full of tough Canadian Black Devils. Through the bulletproof glass of the portholes in the side, Chisnall saw the Demons' vehicle rumble forward; then there was a lurch and they began to follow.

Chisnall put his head back against the headrest, shutting his eyes. Waves of exhaustion swept over him. He had tried to sleep on the submarine the previous day, but even with the help of sleeping tablets, it had not come easily. The whole night had been one of constant tension and hard physical slog, and this was the first time since they had launched from the submarine that he hadn't had to be on the utmost alert, every sense, every brain cell operating at maximum to try and achieve the impossible.

Now his brain was trying to shut down, to rest and repair itself. As was his body. The body armor had saved him from a number of bullets in the forest, but the impact of the bullets had left huge painful bruises. He had new armor on now, as the last was shattered and useless. His ribs were aching but manageable, thanks to some painkillers, which Monster had supplied. Perhaps they were contributing to the waves of sleep that now flooded through his brain.

The MPC quickly picked up speed. The operation's planners had always known it would be a race to get to Lowood once the veil of secrecy was lifted, and after the delays at the river, time was now the critical issue. They had to reach Lowood before the Bzadians could mobilize their defenses.

It was a race to the finish.

■ ■ ■

Price watched Chisnall on the other side of the MPC. He had been sleeping for a while, his chest rising and falling rhythmically, his mouth slightly open. He was even snoring, although it was more of a mild purr than a deep growl like her father's.

"Death to Azoh?" the Tsar said. "What was that all about, Wilton?"

Price smiled to herself. Somehow, at the time, in the smoky thunder of the battle in the forest, it had seemed appropriate.

"I just said the first thing that came to mind." Wilton laughed, too, a little embarrassed.

"You wild man," the Tsar said. "I like it!" He reached over for a high five. "Death to Azoh!"

"Death to Azoh," Price murmured.

"Do you even know what Azoh is?" Barnard asked.

"I'm sure you're going to tell us," Price said.

"Some kind of Puke god," the Tsar said.

"It's the Puke leader," Wilton said.

Barnard shook her head.

"Who cares? Death to Azoh, whoever he is, and thank our God for the Demons back in the forest," the Tsar said.

"It shouldn't have got to that stage," Price said. "It wouldn't have if we'd had real bullets."

"It would not have got to that stage if the LT had let me run the forward fire control and concentrated on defending our position," Barnard said.

There was an icy silence.

"Shut it, Barnard," Price said. "The problem was the bullets, not the LT." *Mostly.*

"Stupid tree-hugging lefties," Wilton said. "Give me some real bullets, an M110, and put me within half a klick of Azoh. War's over, we all go home, and I get to star in Hollywood movies about my life."

"Which shows how little you understand about Azoh," Barnard said.

Chisnall's eyes opened at that point and he looked vaguely around the cabin before they slid shut again.

The vehicle was built for eighteen, and there were only six of them, so there was plenty of space. Price thought about laying Chisnall down across a few seats but worried that doing so would wake him up.

She reached over and switched off his comm so it wouldn't disturb him.

Monster was watching her, and he gave her a smile and nod of approval. She looked away without returning the smile. There was no point in encouraging him.

The Tsar was watching her too. "Is the Big Dog asleep?" he asked.

"Lieutenant Chisnall is asleep, yes," Price said. "And he deserves it."

"No argument from me," the Tsar said. "No need to leap to his defense." He unhooked his weapon and checked the ammunition. "You really like him, don't you?"

"What are you saying?" Price asked.

"Not like that," the Tsar said, reloading his weapon. "I just meant you've known him a long time and you like him."

"He does his job. I do mine," Price said.

"Sounds a bit harsh," the Tsar said. "I thought you were friends."

"I get on fine with him," Price said. "But take a tip, newbie. Don't get too close to anyone. They might not be around all that long."

"Good advice, sweetheart, but I ain't no newbie," the Tsar said.

"No, you're the Hero of Hokkaido," Barnard said.

"Oh, sure, you can spit on it if you want to," the Tsar said, "but I earned that medal."

"Yeah, well, Price won the VC at Uluru, but you don't hear her shouting about it," Wilton said.

"What's that, some little New Zealand medal?" the Tsar said.

"Yeah, just some little New Zealand medal," Price said without looking up.

"No—" Wilton started.

"Just leave it at that," Price said, glaring at him.

"Whatever," the Tsar said. "But I ain't no newbie. I—"

Whatever he was about to say, he never got the chance. His words were cut off midsentence by the sound of an explosion from the front of the convoy. Then another.

And another.

17. MINEFIELD

[0745 hours local time]
[Haigslea Forest, New Bzadia]

"TURN IT AROUND! TURN IT AROUND!" CHISNALL YELLED.

"I'm trying!" the driver yelled back through the grille.

The way ahead was blocked. The column was at a standstill and at the mercy of attackers, hidden deep within the forest on either side. Fairbrother had given the order to retreat, to reverse their course and get out of the ambush that the forest had become.

Another explosion sounded from the head of the column, a thunderclap and a momentary flash of light that coincided with screams on the comm. Thick, oily black smoke billowed, a pungent aroma of death.

The MPCs' turrets were swiveling, and a torrent of bullets was pouring into the forest. Trees shuddered. Some toppled.

The tanks' big guns boomed, over and over again, but the firing from the forest did not diminish.

"Come on!" Chisnall yelled.

The big tires spun, gripped, and the back end fishtailed a little as the MPC headed back down the road. They were following the Canadian Black Devils, who had been the rearguard of the convoy and who were now, by virtue of the turn, the lead vehicle.

To the left and the right of the MPC, the forest was spitting fire and metal. The sides of the MPC rang constantly from the impact of the rounds. Through the grille and out through the windshield, Chisnall could see the Canadian MPC shuddering as heavy machine-gun rounds slammed into it.

The thick glass of the porthole beside his head cracked and starred, once, twice, three times. He ducked instinctively. Hot shell casings landed on the roof as the thudding sound of the fifty-cal came from above them.

"How did they know we were coming through there?" Price asked, her coil-gun in her hands, ready to fire but useless inside the MPC. For a second Chisnall wished the vehicle had gunports, like on old sailing ships, so they could return fire instead of sitting uselessly inside the vehicle.

"I don't know," Chisnall said.

"Why were we taking tanks through a forest?" Barnard asked. "You don't take tanks through a forest if there's another option. Basic tactics! Tanks are easy targets when the enemy can get up close. Why were we going that way? We could have gone around."

"I don't know that either," Chisnall said.

The porthole by his head shattered, blowing glass across the inside of the vehicle. Price ducked, protecting her face with her arm. One direct hit too many, Chisnall thought. The glass could only take so much. He hoped the armored sides of the vehicle would fare better.

He glanced up at the broken window. Now it *was* a gun-port. Chisnall stood, aiming his coil-gun out the window, and ripped off an entire magazine into the forest. Whether he hit anything he didn't know. The explosion and the screech of tires were simultaneous as the wheels of the MPC locked up. Peering through the small metal grille at the front of the vehicle, Chisnall caught a glimpse of the Canadian MPC in midair, fire and smoke billowing underneath it as it landed on shredded tires.

"Mines!" Monster yelled as their own vehicle slewed to one side.

The Angels were thrown forward. Barnard's helmet smashed into Chisnall's head, and only his own helmet saved him from a knockout blow. The back of the MPC lifted as it braked. Chisnall had just enough time to wonder how the Bzadians had managed to lay a minefield so quickly, and how lucky they were not to have hit one, when there was a roar and a flash of heat and light from the front of the vehicle and flames shot through the grille. In slow motion, the world turned topsy-turvy and smoke was everywhere and there was a leg lying over his face.

The MPC was on its side. He could tell from the seats that

had appeared on the ceiling and the fact that he was now lying on his back.

It was Price's leg that covered his face and he was greatly relieved when it moved.

"Monster! Monster!" he yelled, unable to see his friend through the smoke. Talking, however, forced him to breathe, and breathing brought in lung-gripping mouthfuls of acrid black air, choking him.

"The Monster is here." Monster surged past him, to the rear of the MPC.

"Angel Team, status check!" Chisnall yelled, and got a chorus of "Oscar Kilo."

"What about the driver?" he asked. Price was already up by the grille peering through. She shook her head.

"Are you sure?" Chisnall asked, clambering in that direction to look for himself.

Price stopped him with a firm hand on his shoulder. "Don't, Ryan. It's not something you want to see," she said.

The lights inside the MPC flickered a couple of times, then went out, but a hammering sound came from the rear of the vehicle and light and fresh air poured in as Monster wrenched and kicked the buckled rear ramp open.

Wilton clambered to the door and pushed past Monster, who grabbed him by the collar and jerked him back inside, saving him from a volley of Bzadian bullets that would have taken his head off.

The Demon's MPC was behind them and the fifty-cal on the roof was pouring fire into the surrounding forest. But the gap between the vehicles was widening. The MPC was reversing, following its own tire marks back out of the minefield.

"Hey! Hey!" Chisnall yelled, sheltering behind the now-vertical rear ramp.

The Demons came to a halt about a hundred feet from the Angels. A hundred feet that might as well have been a hundred miles. Chisnall knew they would be dead before they made it halfway to the other MPC. Even if they made it, the entry ramp was on the far side of the vehicle. It was suicide to try to get there.

But where else could they go? The Demons' vehicle was the closest refuge from the hail of gunfire around them.

Varmint's voice came in on the Angel channel. "Get over here!"

"We'll never make it!" Chisnall yelled. "You get over here!"

"We can't! It's a minefield!" Varmint yelled. "You come here!"

"We'll never make it!" Chisnall yelled again.

Varmint must have thought so, too, as he didn't try to argue. The MPC began to reverse a little more.

"Varmint, you coward!" Chisnall yelled, but then realized his mistake. The MPC was turning, a quick one-eighty to bring the rear of the vehicle—the ramp, and safety—around to face the Angels.

The ramp of the vehicle was already half-lowered and Varmint was in the rear doorway, one hand on the door edge, one hand on his coil-gun, ignoring the incoming rounds, laying down covering fire. Whatever he was, he was no coward.

"Come on! Come on! Get in here!" Varmint yelled.

"Get closer!" Chisnall yelled back.

"Come on!" Varmint yelled.

"Get closer!" Chisnall yelled again.

"Don't be such a little girl!" Varmint yelled. But that was the last thing he said before the MPC disappeared.

It happened so quickly that it was merely an imprint on the mind's eye, and it was only afterward, when Chisnall ran the scene back in his head, that he could see clearly what happened.

The Demons' MPC executing a three-point turn on the narrow country road.

The ramp that was half-open, exposing the innards of the armored beast.

The streak of light from the edge of the forest. An RPG that should have bounced off the reactive armored sides of the MPC.

The whistle of air as it rocketed past Varmint, through the open doorway, right inside the MPC.

The endless moment that was only a fraction of a second when it appeared the round had been a dud.

The white space and white noise that filled the exact same space where the MPC had been, as the rocket detonated the Demons' demolition charges.

The blinding light that was gone in an instant as the buckled ramp of the Angels' vehicle slammed shut, protecting them from the worst of the blast.

The explosion shunted them forward and, somehow, Chisnall found time to be afraid that they would hit another mine.

When the roar and the incredible blast of superheated air subsided, Monster kicked open the ramp door again, and they stared out at the crater where the Demons' MPC had been. At the hole in the road. At the void in the universe.

"Azoh," Barnard managed.

The others, including Chisnall, were too stunned to speak.

A curious lull had settled over the forest after the explosion, their attackers also stunned or knocked unconscious by the shock wave rippling out through the trees.

"Azoh!" Barnard said again.

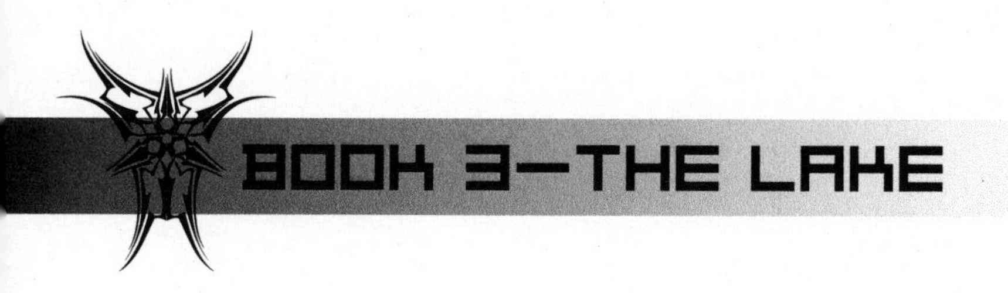
BOOK 3—THE LAKE

18. KOMMANDOS

BY 08:00 HOURS, OPERATION MAGNUM WAS IN TROUBLE.

The Haigslea Forest ambush by a relatively small force from the Borallon Defense Barracks had stopped the task force in its tracks.

The Bzadian defenders had laid antitank mines ahead of the convoy and had also mined the road behind the task force once they had passed in order to block their retreat. The task force was trapped and under heavy fire.

It was the German Kommando Spezialkrafte who saved the day. The doors of their MPCs were open before the vehicles had stopped moving and the elite German special forces soldiers melted into the forest.

The Bzadians found themselves in a fierce gunfight among the trees, which halted the attack on the convoy and allowed the rest of the task force soldiers to dismount and follow the Kommandos.

The fighting was brutal, and sometimes tree to tree. The smoke from the burning tanks was so dense that a human and a Bzadian could be on opposite sides of the same tree and not know the other was there. Some of the Kommandos put away their guns entirely and drew their knives, slipping through the forest like ghosts.

The fierce fighting amid the smoke-shrouded trees continued for over an hour before the Bzadians were forced back deep enough into the forest for a mine-clearing team to secure a path.

The convoy, now comprising just seven tanks and fifty-nine of the original seventy MPCs, headed south out of the forest, then north, across open farmland.

Finally, they were back on their original course, but the operation, already an hour behind schedule, was delayed another hour. Hours that would prove crucial in the battle to come.

19. BAD TIMING

[MISSION DAY 2]
[0910 hours local time]
[Northwest of Haigslea Forest, New Bzadia]

THE MPC BUMPED AND BOUNCED OVER THE UNDULATING farmland, cutting across country to get to the highway, skirting around the killing zone of the Haigslea Forest.

The Angels were in the rear of Task Force Actual, the command vehicle. So many vehicles had been knocked out in the forest that it was the only free space. Unlike most MPCs, it was divided into two sections, with a command module at the front and seating at the rear. Colonel Fairbrother and three command center staff were busy on the radios, consulting maps and monitoring views from aerial cameras that flew over the convoy in tiny, hand-launched drones.

The Angels sat in the back. They watched each other,

unwilling to speak, the silence growing into a rigid wall between them.

Barnard was the first to break it. "What a moron," she said.

"I thought he was brave," Wilton said after a moment.

"He was stupid," Barnard said. "Just a dumb grunt. Drawing fire like that."

"He saved our lives," Price said.

"Dumb Pukehead," Barnard said.

"I'd have done the same," the Tsar said.

"Oh, you're such a hero," Barnard said.

"I think I would too," Wilton said.

"Yeah, really?" Barnard said. "You'd give up your own life to save these guys? Don't be an idiot. They don't even like you very much."

"That's not true, Wilton," Price said. "Don't listen to her."

"I would, if it came down to it, yeah," Wilton said.

"Why would you do that?" Barnard asked. "Get yourself killed. Why would anyone do that?"

"Great men are always prepared to lay down their lives for their country, or their planet," the Tsar said.

"You're not a great man," Barnard said. "You're not even a man. Not yet."

"Can it, Barnard!" Chisnall said.

Barnard had taken off a combat glove and was wiping at her eyes. When she took her hand away, they were dry but red-rimmed. "And I suppose the same goes for you, Wilton," she said. "Are you a great man?"

"I'm no hero," Wilton said.

"Then why?" Barnard asked.

"It's just, you know," Wilton said, with a slightly embarrassed look around at the others, "we've been through a lot together."

"So what?" Barnard asked.

"I wouldn't want to let them down," Wilton said.

"You'd rather die first?" Barnard asked.

"If I had to," Wilton said.

"Boo-yah," Monster said quietly.

Barnard considered that for a moment, staring at Wilton. He turned away, uncomfortable under her gaze.

"I still think you're an idiot, Wilton," Barnard said. The corners of her lips curled upward in a rare smile. "But not all the time."

"You knew Varmint somehow, didn't you?" Chisnall asked Barnard.

"John. His name was John," Barnard said. "He wasn't the idiot you guys seem to think."

He wasn't an idiot at all, Chisnall thought. *Far from it.*

"Barnard, were you and he . . . ?" Price asked.

"No, I told you. Nothing like that. It was . . ." Barnard stopped and took a deep breath. "It was on the voyage out. I was wandering around the ship. It was late." She paused, and there was silence except for the growl of the engine and the rumble of the tires on the rough ground. "I was up on the deck. I ran into three of the Russians." She carefully avoided the Tsar's eyes. "They were drunk."

"Drunk?" Chisnall asked.

"Must have smuggled something on board," Price said.

"They cornered me," Barnard said. "Asked me for a kiss."

"A kiss?" Wilton asked.

"They were egging each other on. Said it was the closest they'd ever get to kissing a real Puke."

"So I gave them some lip, which pissed them off. Then I tried to push past them, but suddenly it was vodka breath and hands everywhere. There were three of them, and they were a lot bigger than me," Barnard said.

"Jeez!" the Tsar said.

"It was going badly, if you know what I mean, and the next minute someone else was there, laying into them."

"Varmint?" Chisnall asked.

Barnard nodded. "I don't know where he came from but that evened up the odds a bit."

"They're real tough, those Spetsnaz guys," the Tsar said.

"Maybe, but they were drunk, I was angry, and Varmint was one hard-ass son of a bitch." Barnard said it matter-of-factly. "It was pretty even. Then a squad of Kommandos turned up, out for a training run. The Russians disappeared real fast."

"Why wasn't this reported?" Chisnall asked.

"On the eve of the operation? What good would it have done? We're all on a suicide mission anyway. Put it down to bad vodka and worse timing."

"Why didn't you tell *me*?" Chisnall asked.

"You would have reported it," Barnard said.

"I . . ." Chisnall stopped himself. She was probably right.

"What do you mean, a suicide mission?" Price asked.

"You figure it out," Barnard said.

"Freaking Russians," Wilton said, then glanced at the Tsar. "I mean . . ."

"Don't judge all of us by the actions of a few," the Tsar said.

Barnard reached across to the other side of the vehicle and put her hand on the Tsar's knee. The action surprised Chisnall in its intimacy. It clearly surprised the Tsar as well. As she continued to hold his knee, without speaking, he grew more and more uncomfortable, but she did not remove her hand.

"I don't judge you by them," Barnard said eventually. "I judge you by you."

The Tsar held her gaze.

"I know what happened at Hokkaido," she said.

The Tsar said nothing, still holding her gaze.

"I know and I don't care," Barnard said. "Just stop pretending you're a hero."

All eyes were on the Tsar, and he stiffened and straightened.

"I've got news for you, sweetheart," the Tsar said. "I'm not pretending. We could use a little more of that around here." This last was followed by a pointed glance at Chisnall.

A low growl came from Monster's throat.

"Be very careful what you say from now on," Price said.

"Go easy. Maybe he's right," Chisnall said.

"Not in my book," Wilton said.

Barnard let go of the Tsar's knee and leaned back in her seat.

"Yeah, Tsar, you're a hero," Barnard said. "The kind of hero who gets other people killed. Chisnall, he's the kind of hero who's doing his damn best to get everyone home alive."

Chisnall looked up, surprised that Barnard would stick up for him like that.

"It's not about us surviving. It's about completing the mission," the Tsar said. "If the LT can't see that, then maybe he's not the man for the job."

"Who is? You? Forget it," Barnard said. "These guys love Chisnall. Look at them. They would never follow you. In fact, they think you might be a traitor."

"That's not true," Chisnall said.

"Really?" Barnard said. "You thought I was."

Chisnall opened his mouth to reply but shut it again. She was right.

"Why would you accuse me of that?" There was surprise and anger in the Tsar's voice, and Chisnall didn't think he was acting.

"You gotta wonder who tampered with the Demons' sonar," Price said.

She refrained from pointing out that the Tsar was their communications and sonar specialist.

"Not me," the Tsar said. "Someone at the naval base? Maybe it got knocked when it was loaded onto the sub. Maybe it's just some faulty two-dollar computer chip." He stared around at the other members of the team. "Why would you even think that?"

"We thought the Pukes might have captured your family," Chisnall said. "That they could be using them against you."

The Tsar shut his eyes, swaying a little in his seat. He seemed suddenly a long way away.

"They're not holding my family," he said.

"And I'm sure there's a way of proving that," Price said.

"There's nothing to prove," the Tsar said. "My mother and father were killed at Volgograd." He took a deep breath and continued without opening his eyes. "I had two sisters and a little brother. My aunt tried to get us out. Pukes stopped us at the border, did some kind of eeny-meeny-miny-mo thing and let me through."

"What happened to the others?" Price asked.

The Tsar finally opened his eyes and looked around the cabin. "I don't know. I heard shots. I wanted to go back, but . . . I didn't want to go back." He dropped his head into his hands.

"Jeez," he said, "I was only twelve."

20. WARREGO HIGHWAY

[0940 hours local time]
[Warrego Highway, New Bzadia]

PLANS HAD CHANGED.

Without the Demons, the Angels had become the backup plan, tasked with destroying the generators at Splityard Creek. They were all issued with packs of high explosive. As for Reservoir Hill, in Fairbrother's words: "That'll just have to bloody take care of itself."

One part of the plan hadn't changed. Finding transport.

Fairbrother had dropped them a mile away from the produce market. They tabbed across farmland that was thick and choking with a strange Bzadian herb. The air was heady with the scent of the flowers that grew at the top of long stalks and from the pungent aroma of the thick leaves.

"Stinks like Monster's farts," Wilton said at one point.

Chisnall was almost ready to vomit when they finally

reached a lane between two fields. Although the path was narrow and winding, enough clear air fell into the gap to relieve the nausea. They made good time along the lane, for all its winding bends, and only slowed down when they reached the Warrego Highway.

Chisnall eased aside two stalks of the plant and fixed his eyes on the buildings on the other side of the highway. At one end, a small petrol station looked clean, and well used. Nobody was visible either inside or outside the small office to the rear. To the left of the office was a fruit and vegetable shop, but the sign had fallen into disrepair so that it said "Fruit & V." The windows of the shop were broken. It appeared deserted. More produce shops and a couple of sheds completed the road-stop produce stand, but if anybody still lived or worked here, there was no sign of them.

"Anything on the scope?" he asked.

"Some rotorcraft activity out to the east, seems to be heading our way," the Tsar said. "If we're going to scoot across the highway, we'd better do it soon."

"Attack craft?" Chisnall asked.

"I don't think so," the Tsar said. "There's only three of them. I'd guess reconnaissance."

"Okay, let's do it," Chisnall said. "Be casual. We're a bunch of Puke soldiers out to buy some lunch."

"If this is what they sell," Price said, pushing a stalk away from her face, "I'll go hungry."

Chisnall broke cover and trotted across the highway, the others behind him, weapons holstered, their body language nonthreatening. As he ran, he was suddenly conscious of the

C4 pack on his back. It wasn't a nice feeling to be attached to a few kilos of high explosive. Especially after what happened to the Demons. He pushed the thought out of his mind.

It was pretty obvious as soon as they reached the buildings that appearances were not deceptive. The buildings were empty and unused. A driveway led between the buildings to a large old house, which also seemed deserted.

In a parking area were four vehicles: two cars, a four-wheel drive, and a station wagon, clearly the transportation that Fairbrother had told them about.

"Check them out," Chisnall said.

Monster nodded and moved to the four-wheel drive. Wilton went with him.

"Scout around," Chisnall said to the others. The strangeness was upon him. That indefinable feeling he got when something wasn't right. "Make sure there's nobody hiding anywhere."

He walked up to the front door and pushed it open, drawing his pistol as he did so.

The entranceway was empty, dusty. The house had not been lived in for many years. It led to a family room, then to a dining room, also empty.

He found them in the kitchen, seated at a table as if they were about to start lunch. But lunch was never coming. They had been dead so long that they were no more than skeletons, with a few remaining scraps of flesh waiting for the insects and microbes to eat and rot them away.

A human family. Two adults and four young children. The bullet holes in their skulls mute evidence to what had happened.

The why would probably never be known. They were not soldiers, just a farming family running a produce stand. Why hadn't they left? Maybe they were not given the chance. Maybe something had happened here that the Bzadian soldiers who committed the atrocity had not wanted the world to know about.

Chisnall left the way he had come and pulled the front door shut behind him.

"Anything in there?" Price asked, arriving around the corner of the house.

"Nothing," Chisnall said. And it was nothing. Just one more senseless slaughter in a war that was nothing but senseless slaughter. "Where are those rotorcraft?" he asked.

"Bypassed us to the south," the Tsar said. "All clear."

"Okay, good," Chisnall said. "How're the cars?" This to Monster, who was shutting the hood of the station wagon.

"Lump-solid rusted." He shook his head and pointed at both of the cars. "She and her."

"Jeez, Monster, learn to speak bloody English," Price said.

"The Monster's English is goodly spoken," Monster said.

"Well, mine must be awful, then, because I can't understand a word you're saying," Price said.

"My English still better than your Hungarian," Monster said with a smile.

"Can't argue with that," the Tsar said.

"Who needs to speak Hungarian?" Price said. "No . . ."

She stopped herself, but Chisnall knew what she had been going to say next. "Nobody speaks that anymore." Not since the invasion. Hungary, as a country, had ceased to exist. He saw Monster's shoulders tense.

"Come on, kids," Chisnall said. "Play nice." The bickering seemed especially petty, considering what he had found in the kitchen. "So the cars are kaput?"

"The cars are kaput," Monster said, enunciating each word carefully.

"Damn," the Tsar said. "It's a long walk to Splityard Creek."

"Maybe not," Wilton said on the comm. "Barn—just left of the house."

The barn was intact, and weatherproof, which may have had something to do with the state of the motorcycles and quad bikes inside. There were two quads and three motorcycles, each dirty, dusty, and rusted. Surface rust only, Chisnall thought, and Monster quickly confirmed it. A few minutes' fiddling with some wires and one of the dirt bikes coughed, choked, then spluttered into life.

"We'll need gas," Chisnall said. He nodded at Wilton. "See what you can find at that gas station back on the road."

Wilton disappeared.

Monster went over all the bikes. He was happy with two of the quad bikes and one of the dirt bikes. The second dirt bike he made a face at and kicked off its stand. It lay on the floor, its back wheel rusted. The last dirt bike would not start, but Monster found a can of oil on a shelf at the back of the barn and finally coaxed it to life, just as Wilton arrived back with two jerry cans and a strong smell of petrol.

"You been drinking the stuff?" Price asked.

"It's been a while since I learned how to siphon," Wilton said, and spat onto the floor of the barn.

"What, you couldn't find any cars to steal at Fort Carson?" Price asked.

"What can I say? I was young and stupid," Wilton said.

"Wow, you've really changed," Barnard said.

"How did you know?" Wilton asked, turning to Price. "Those court records were supposed to be sealed, because I was a juvenile."

"I just guessed," Price said.

While Wilton filled the petrol tanks, Chisnall motioned Monster to follow him and stepped outside the barn. The niggling between him and Price had been going on for too long, and he needed them focused on the mission.

"What's with you and Price?" he asked, off comm.

"Is nothing, LT."

"Seriously?"

Monster shrugged. "Back at Carson, after Uluru, we kind of, you know, got together."

"You and Price?"

Chisnall wasn't sure whether to be surprised, happy for them, or miffed that Monster had kept this a secret from him.

"Like beast and the beauty." Monster laughed. "Maybe she just need someone for leaning on."

"We all did," Chisnall said. "But you kept it quiet."

"Against regulations. You know this."

Chisnall almost smiled. His own disastrous "against regulations" romance with Holly Brogan was not a secret in the Angel Team. "What happened?" he asked.

"One minute she warm like summer, next minute she cold like winter."

"No reason?"

"Maybe the Monster say something wrong, I don't know."

"You okay about it?" Chisnall asked. There was a pause.

"Everything is the way it is meant to be," Monster said finally.

"Okay, make an effort, big guy. I don't need the stress."

Monster nodded and moved off.

"Like beast and the beauty," Chisnall murmured to himself.

He had known Monster for more than three years but had never guessed at this side of him. Beneath the coarse, jovial exterior, behind the mystic mutterings, there was a heart that, if not exactly broken, was cracked and bleeding.

A few moments later, petrol tanks filled, they were on their way. Price drove one of the quad bikes, with Wilton grinning cheerfully on the back. The Tsar and Monster took the dirt bikes, while Barnard waited for Chisnall to get onto the second quad before flinging a leg over behind him.

"Want to drive?" Chisnall asked. "My ribs are still giving me hell."

"Up to you," Barnard said. "But I need to do some research on those generators if we're going to do this right."

"I'll handle it," Chisnall said. "How's the uplink?" The wrist computers were connected to a comms satellite high above them.

Barnard was tapping buttons. "Slow, but a steady signal," she said.

They took the highway east until they could swing north

onto the Brisbane Valley Highway, which would take them most of the way to the dam.

A rotorcraft overflew them as they approached the half-way mark, near the old Borallon Correctional Facility. Chisnall avoided looking up as it hovered low over them. *Just a squad of soldiers on a patrol,* he said to himself. The quads and dirt bikes were not a problem. Bzadians used left-behind human equipment and vehicles all the time.

The rotorcraft took off to the west, in the direction of Lowood.

Chisnall turned his attention back to the road, and another couple of miles slipped by.

The calm of the countryside was finally broken by the sound of fighting to their west. The far-off boom of explosions rumbled over the scrub and hills. The initial exchange was followed by a constant patter of gunfire, and it was clear that the task force was getting into a major battle. In the distance, plumes of smoke rose into the air.

"We have a problem," Barnard said.

Even with the comm it was hard to hear her over the buzz-saw growling of the quad bike. Chisnall glanced back at her. She had been silent, working on her wrist computer the entire way.

"What is it?" he asked.

"There's a second generator," Barnard said.

"What do you mean a second generator?" Price asked.

"Exactly that," Barnard said. "The hydroelectric generators we're going to destroy are at the base of Splityard Creek. They're the main power generators for the dam, but they're not the only ones. A second generator plant was installed in 2003 beneath one of the spillways."

"So we destroy that too," Wilton said, pulling up alongside them and grinning.

"We'd never get near it," Barnard said. "Weren't you listening? It's beneath one of the spillways. We'd have to rappel down the face of the dam to get to it, and that's not possible."

"Not with the Pukes keeping watch," Chisnall agreed. "So why have they even sent us on this mission? Why send the Demons in the first place?"

"It's just another cluster muck-up. Like always," Barnard said. "Bad planning, bad decisions."

"Let me check it out," Chisnall said.

If Barnard was right, then this whole part of the mission was a waste of time, and a needless risk. And Barnard, so far, had been right about everything.

He switched to the command channel.

"Angel One to Task Force Actual. How copy?"

"Solid copy, Angel One, but we're a little busy here."

An explosion boomed over the radio, and a second later Chisnall heard the same blast vibrating across the farm fields to his left.

"Urgent interrogational, Task Force Actual. We are showing a second generator at Wivenhoe. Taking out the main plant may not be enough. How do you want us to proceed? Over."

There was a moment's silence; then Fairbrother's voice came on the channel. He had to shout to be heard over the gunfire in the background.

"Angel One, we are aware of the second generator, but it has no significance. Its power output is too low. Proceed with the attack as planned, and don't use this channel unless it's an emergency. How copy, Angel One?"

"Solid copy, Task Force Actual."

Chisnall clicked off the channel. "They knew about the second generator," he said, "but it's not important. It's not big enough to power Lowood."

"Turnoff to Splityard Creek coming up in one klick," Price said.

"He's wrong," Barnard said.

"A bunch of experts have studied that dam," Chisnall said. "He's not wrong."

"Yes, he is," Barnard said. "You have to understand Bzadian psychology."

"And how do you know so much about that subject?" the Tsar asked.

"I studied it at Stanford University," she said.

"You're talking out of your butt," the Tsar said. "You've been in Angel training since you were thirteen. You never had time to go to Stanford. You think you're real smart, but you're just a grunt like the rest of us."

"I passed my SATs at twelve," Barnard said, without false modesty. "I applied for psych at Stanford and got accepted. I'd be there now if they hadn't recruited me. That's the truth, whether you believe it or not."

"You know what I think?" the Tsar said. "I think you dispense bull like you invented it and own the rights."

"I don't give a fat rat what you think," Barnard said. "But if I did, trust me, you'd be the first person I'd give it to."

"What aren't you telling us?" Chisnall asked. "Who recruited you from Stanford? Recon Team Angel?"

Barnard shook her head. "It doesn't matter."

Chisnall stared at her. It did matter. It mattered a lot. But it was clear that she had no intention of saying.

"So what are you doing here?" Price asked.

"Firsthand experience," Barnard said. "They want us to get inside the Pukes' minds, to help figure out how to win this war. Couldn't do that sitting in an office in the Pentagon, so here I am."

"You had an office at the Pentagon?" Wilton said. "Cool!"

"And how does this apply to the generators?" Chisnall asked.

"The psychology of social structures," Barnard said.

"We think of ourselves as individuals; then we form groups like this team, or a community, or a country. But Pukes think the opposite way around."

"What the heck are you talking about?" the Tsar asked.

"About Azoh," Barnard said.

"Their god?" Wilton asked.

"Azoh's not a god. It's a collective intelligence that the Pukes believe in. They see themselves as tiny parts of one whole."

"Like ants," Chisnall said.

"Like ants," Barnard agreed.

"Don't ants have a queen?" Wilton asked.

"Yes, and so do the Pukes," Barnard said.

"Azoh," Chisnall said.

"The 'brain' of this collective intelligence is one individual, and they worship him or her as we worship our gods. This individual is known as Azoh, even though Azoh actually refers to all living Bzadians."

"Do Pukes really have a common mind?" Price asked. "Like ants. Is that true?"

"It's true that they believe it. It's like a religion," Barnard said. "There's no proof. But that doesn't stop them believing."

"What has this got to do with the generators?" Chisnall asked.

"Okay. The generators at Wivenhoe power half of Brisbane," Barnard said. "Much of it essential services. Keeping hospitals running. Keeping patients alive. If this were a human country, they'd have to keep those facilities operating. Pukes don't think like that. The needs of the collective intelligence come first. Everything else comes second. Azoh is more important than the individual. Funny thing is, some Puke soldier, dying on a hospital bed for a lack of electricity, would totally get that. They would understand their place in the overall scheme of things. And if their place is to die, then they will die."

"Even if that's all true, it doesn't change anything," Chisnall said. "The secondary generator produces less than half the electricity the fuel plant needs."

"So they'll produce less than half their normal output of fuel cells," Barnard said. "That might slow down the invasion of the Free Territories, but it won't stop it."

"Do you have a better idea?" Chisnall asked.

"No," Barnard said. "But I'm working on it."

21. YOZI

[1000 hours local time]
[Warrego Highway, New Bzadia]

THE HUM OF THE MASSIVE ROTOR BLADES BENEATH them was a comforting and familiar sound. There were no windows, but the central video screens showed the world outside. The lines of rotorcraft streaking low above the ground in a tight formation, trying to stay below enemy radar.

The squad members, particularly the new recruits, some of them just out of the military academy, were excitable and chattering.

Yozi shared a glance with Alizza, who gave him a crooked-toothed grin. New images were appearing on the screens now. Footage from the reconnaissance craft that were approaching the invaders, staying out of reach of the sting in the tail of their javelin missiles.

The younger soldiers stopped talking and watched the

screens. White flashes of explosions were like pinpricks in the high-altitude shots, and parts of the picture were obscured by wreaths of smoke. Other screens showed closer angles of the battle, and as they watched, a spiraling trail of smoke streaked down from a hillside, scoring a direct hit on a human tank, which erupted in flames. A fierce firefight was taking place on the riverbank, younger soldiers cheering at the bravery of the defenders, until two amphibious human craft rose up from the water, chewing up the defensive position with heavy machine-gun fire.

The footage changed to that from another recon craft, this time showing a view from the west, the direction in which they were traveling. From this angle, Yozi could see that most of the fighting centered on one hill, which commanded the approach roads. Reinforcing that hill would be his top priority once on the ground. The defenders looked in danger of being overwhelmed, and Yozi fumed that his squad was still over an hour away.

One of the screens showed the view from a third recon rotorcraft traveling toward Lowood from the east. It passed over a squad of Bzadian soldiers on powered cycle transport, human vehicles, heading along a highway.

"Run that again," Alizza grunted.

Yozi looked at his friend. Alizza's eyes were still fixed on the screen, although it now showed nothing but empty fields.

He tapped the intercom for the flight crew. "Back up the video on screen three. The soldiers on the motor bicycles."

With a brief acknowledgment from the flight deck, the video began to reverse, pausing on the soldiers.

“A little more,” Alizza said, and Yozi repeated the request to the flight deck.

“Stop.”

One of the soldiers had glanced up at the rotorcraft. The face was only a pale dot on the screen, but something had triggered Alizza’s interest.

“Zoom in on the soldiers,” Yozi said, and the four shapes on the highway began to grow, resolving into six clear images. They were looking down on the soldiers and could not see their faces. Except for one, frozen in time, looking up at the camera.

“Is it him?” Alizza asked.

Yozi checked the screen again to be sure. It was blurred, but he was sure. It might have been the wide shoulders that went with the face.

“Yes, it’s him,” Yozi said.

It was one of the team that had defeated them at Uluru. The team led by Chizna. It was the large one. The one they called Monster. With a cold, hard certainty in his heart, he knew that Chizna was on one of the other powered cycles.

“Which way are they headed?” Alizza asked.

“North,” Yozi said. “To the dam.”

22. WIVENHOE

[1010 hours local time]
[Lake Wivenhoe, New Bzadia]

THEY STOPPED THE BIKES ON THE RIDGELINE. TO THEIR right was the small lake at Splityard Creek. Below them, down a steep ravine, was the generating plant they had come to destroy. It extended out from the shore of the main lake in a small inlet. Up here on the ridge there was no security, because there was nothing to attack but a hill.

But the generating plant looked well defended, with double wire fences and two guard stations. A patrol boat with a heavy machine gun mounted on the bow was moored at a small jetty to the left of the plant.

Wivenhoe Dam stretched across the other side of the lake, a massive earthen embankment, imposing its will on the pent-up waters. Even from the opposite shore, at least three miles away, the dam was impressive. It had to be; it was holding back a million megaliters of water, twice the amount of water in Sydney Harbor.

A side road a hundred meters back led down to the plant, but Chisnall had wanted to reconnoiter the site first, and the high ridgeline was the ideal place to do it.

Across the lake, the dam looked even better defended. A tall gantry crane in the center of the dam bristled with weapons. The Bzadians might not have been expecting an attack here in their heartland, but they were certainly well prepared.

"Let's get down there," Chisnall said. "Follow my lead. We'll bluff our way as far as we can, but be prepared to go hot and loud in a hurry. The action word, as usual, is *dingo*."

"Major Kriz, I am Yozi," the voice said in her headset. She could hear the hum of a rotorcraft engine in the background.

"Yozi? Where are you?" Kriz asked.

"En route to Lowood," Yozi said.

"Lowood, why?" Kriz asked. As far as she knew, Yozi was a command center supervisor, not a combat soldier.

"It doesn't matter," Yozi said. "I have vital information for you."

"Speak," Kriz said.

"We have identified a team of scumbugz heading for the dam at Wivenhoe," Yozi said. "They are disguised as Bzadians."

"You're sure?" Kriz asked.

"No," Yozi said. "Not sure enough. Can you check if we have any teams on missions in that area?"

"I will get someone on it," Kriz said. "If they are disguised as Bzadians, how did you ID them?"

"From a reconnaissance video. It is not that clear. But if I am right, then some of them were at Uluru during the attack," Yozi said. "The leader is called Chizna."

"Chizel!" Kriz blurted out. *Could it be the same?*

"You know of him?"

"I killed him. At least I shot him. By the river. I thought he was dead."

There was silence while he digested that. When he spoke again, he almost sounded disappointed, Kriz thought.

"I need permission to divert to Wivenhoe," Yozi said.

"Granted," Kriz said, making a note. "What is your rotorcraft designation? I'll send the permission to your pilot."

"And alert the security at Wivenhoe," Yozi said.

"Of course," Kriz said.

A gate guard stopped them with an upraised hand, and three more stood nearby, alert, but not yet drawing weapons. Chisnall dismounted the quad bike as soon as it stopped.

"What are you doing here?" the guard asked.

"I am Chizel. Haven't you heard?" Chisnall said. "Scumbugz have landed in this area. They're only a few miles down the road. We're here to reinforce your security in case they attack the dam."

A female guard captain came out of a guardhouse but made no move to open the gate. "We have no knowledge of this," she said.

"There's an invasion in your area and you know nothing about it?" Chisnall exploded.

"Of course we know about the invasion," the captain said. "But we weren't informed of any reinforcements."

"So what were you planning to do?" Chisnall asked. "Stop an entire army of scumbugz with four soldiers?"

"Six," the captain replied with a slight rise to her voice.

"Well, now we are twelve," Chisnall said. "I hope to Azoh that it is enough, if they head in our direction."

"I will need to get confirmation," the captain said.

"Of course," Chisnall said.

Even as he finished speaking, an alarm siren began to sound from the direction of the dam, clearly audible across the few miles of water, despite the low headland of the inlet. He counted the guards. Two at each guard station, plus the captain. That left one still unaccounted for.

The guard's radio beeped, and she raised it to her ear, listening carefully. She was trying to keep her expression neutral, but there was no mistaking the way her eyes suddenly shot around the Angels and back to Chisnall. She replaced her radio on her belt and kept her hand there, casually—right next to her sidearm.

"Get back on your radio," Chisnall said. "Talk to your regional headquarters. They know we are coming."

The captain raised an eyebrow and her hand inched closer to the butt of her sidearm.

"Our designation is team dingo," Chisnall said.

The captain grabbed at her sidearm, but her chest exploded in puffer smoke. The Tsar had drawn, aimed, and fired before she even loosened it in the holster.

The other Angels were almost as fast. Four Bzadian guards hit the ground simultaneously. A rattle of heavy machine-gun fire made Chisnall dive to the ground, and from the direction of the sound, he guessed it was coming from the boat.

"Get this gate open!" Chisnall yelled.

Price had wire cutters out in a second and began snipping strands, but Monster found a faster way, grasping hold of a bar and lifting the end of the gate up off its hinges, never minding the bullets and tracer rounds that sparked and flashed off the fence around him.

The Angel Team ran through the gap, using several small vehicles as cover. Glass shattered and the cars shuddered as the heavy machine-gun rounds followed them to the parking area by the main building.

"See if you can get an angle on him," Chisnall said to Wilton. "Suppressing fire!" He hurled a smoke grenade. A thick blanket of white smoke hissed and filled the air around them.

The Angels' bullets peppered the smoke as they returned fire toward the jetty. There was a single crack from Wilton's gun and a corresponding splash from down near the boat.

Chisnall stood and hurried down to the jetty, but the Tsar had beaten him to it and was already hauling the unconscious Bzadian out of the water.

"Couldn't let him drown," the Tsar said.

Chisnall thought again of the twelve-year-old boy listening to the gunshots at the Russian border and wondered if he had vastly underestimated the Tsar.

Price had found some keys on the captain's belt and used them to open the main door to the generator plant. Chisnall and Barnard followed her inside.

The noise was overpowering, a roar that was part water sluicing through giant tubes and part the whine of the turbo generators. Barnard went quickly around the room, identifying the machinery. "Generators," she said, pointing at six huge metal boxes, painted an olive green and studded with bolts the size of Chisnall's head. "Inductors, intake tubes, backup power supply."

The last was a long metal device lined with metal tubes the size of 200-liter drums.

"Fuel cells?" Price asked. "I thought this place generated power. Why does it need fuel cells?"

"It makes power by pumping water from the main lake up to the smaller lake above us," Barnard said. "It needs power to run the pumps. It generates its own electricity for the pumps, but if the top lake should ever run dry, they'd need a backup."

"Those fuel cells will go up like a volcano," Chisnall said, remembering the shuddering surface of Uluru. "It'll leave a smoking crater where this plant is."

"But that doesn't solve our problem of the other generator at the dam. If we can't shut that down, then everything, this whole operation, is for nothing."

Chisnall thought of the gantry crane on the dam, heavily armed, and the guards, now alerted to their presence. He shrugged. "Our orders are to blow this one, so that's what we'll do. We'd never get to the other."

"There might be a way," Barnard said.

"Hold that thought," Chisnall said. She had earned the right to a hearing. "Everybody, bring your C4 packs in here. After that, we'd better get ready for company. Monster, see if you can fix that fence you broke. Everybody set up defensive positions. I want clear kill zones and overlapping fields of fire. Are we clear?"

"Barnard, you give me a hand to rig the charges on these fuel cells," Chisnall said. "While we do it, tell me what you're thinking."

Chisnall took a C4 satchel and held it against the nearest fuel cell, a large silver drum, trying to determine the best way to attach it. The satchels came with an assortment of straps and catches for exactly this kind of purpose.

"I've been in contact with some professors at Stanford, experts in fluid dynamics," Barnard said.

"Keep talking," Chisnall said. He laid the C4 satchel flat on top of the cell and found he could attach it securely to the fuel cell's handles with a strap.

"A wave traveling in a liquid, like the sea, can carry a tremendous amount of energy," Barnard said. "Although you can't see it until it hits dry land."

"Like a tsunami," Chisnall said.

"Exactly," Barnard said. "Imagine if you could create a tsunami." She followed Chisnall's lead and attached the first of her satchels in the same manner.

"You'd need an earthquake, or a volcanic eruption," Chisnall said. "We can't do that."

"No, but we could set off an underwater explosion," Barnard said. "That would create a huge pressure wave."

She banged her hand on one of the fuel cells as she spoke, making Chisnall jump, even though he knew they were perfectly safe without an explosion to set them off.

"Still not as big as a tsunami," he said.

"So we set off a series of explosions, timing them exactly so that the waves synchronize." *Bang, bang, bang* on the side of the fuel cell, again making him jump. "They all converge on the same spot at the same time. It's called wave amplification."

"You're talking about taking out the dam," Chisnall realized. "Can that be done?"

"Not without a nuke," Barnard said. She stopped what she was doing and moved over to Chisnall. She brought up a satellite map of the area on her wrist computer. "But look at the gates. These concrete walls would act as a funnel and amplify the power of our 'tsunami' even more, forcing it into a smaller and smaller area. Also, the lake gets shallower as it rises up to meet the dam, which concentrates it further. The gates are designed to resist the weight of the water in the lake, not a sudden destructive blast. If we can take out even one of the gates, Lowood will end up underwater."

"So will the task force," Chisnall said, studying the map.

"Not if we give them enough warning," Barnard said. "Tell them to get clear."

"Okay. I like it," Chisnall said. "But only as a last resort. Only if the task force fails to get through to Lowood."

"I'll ask the Stanford guys to start running the numbers," Barnard said.

Kriz examined her computer screen one more time, analyzing the information, evaluating possibilities.

The humans had attacked Splityard Creek. Clearly they were after the generator station. If they succeeded, that would knock out three-quarters of the power output from the dam. They had to be stopped. The good news was that Yozi and his team were on their way to the dam. There was a quiet assurance and competence about Yozi that gave her some confidence.

A status update flashed up on her screen as she watched. More good news. The squadron from Nambour had made much better time than expected. She smiled to herself. Chizel and his friends were pretty tough against one lightly armed pen pusher. See how they fared against twenty-four giant Bzadian battle tanks.

23. FLUID DYNAMICS

[1030 hours local time]
[Lake Wivenhoe, New Bzadia]

"WILTON, ANYTHING HAPPENING ON THE DAM?" CHISNALL asked.

Wilton was in his favorite position, on the roof of the building, with a good view of the approach road and the surrounding area.

"They're all in a buzz, but they aren't going anywhere," Wilton said. "They're on top of that big crane thing. I reckon they're more worried about defending their own position than trying to attack us."

Chisnall was sure that would change when reinforcements arrived.

He was standing, leaning on one of the quad bikes, unwilling to sit down despite legs that felt like lead. If he sat down, he would have to stand back up, and that was still a mammoth effort, despite the painkillers.

Barnard was sitting cross-legged on the ground, working on her wrist computer. She looked like a kid at school, Chisnall thought. But this was a long way from school.

She stood and walked over to him. "I heard back from Stanford."

"About our tsunami?" Chisnall asked.

"Yes. A bunch of students, with help from a couple of professors, have been running simulations on a computer model. They're not guaranteeing anything, but they say it's theoretically possible."

She waved her computer at him. It contained strings of numbers that meant nothing to Chisnall. "Based on their best calculations, we need to set up three explosions."

"What is that?" he asked, pointing at the computer.

"GPS coordinates, depths, and timing sequence," she said.

"Chances of success?" he asked.

"Better than average," she said. "And a lot better than if we do nothing."

Chisnall nodded.

"But the locations of the explosions in the lake, the depths, and the timing of the detonations all have to be perfect," Barnard said. "It's your call, LT."

"I know, but what's your opinion, Barnard?" Chisnall asked.

"I believe it will work," Barnard said.

Chisnall stared at her for a moment, realizing that in less

than a day, she had gone from someone he hardly knew, and didn't really like, to a person whose fierce intelligence he had come to rely on. If she believed it could be done, there was a good chance she was right. And if she believed that blowing up the generators would not stop production at Lowood, then she was probably right about that also.

"Okay. Let's do it," Chisnall said.

"There's one complication," Barnard said.

"Naturally," Chisnall said.

"The professors are not sure about the power of the wave, the 'tsunami' alone," she said. "There are smaller bulkhead gates that protect the main gates. We need to take out one of the bulkhead gates a few seconds before our tsunami arrives. They think we need one more explosion, right at the face of the dam, ten or fifteen meters down. It more than doubles our chances of success."

Chisnall looked over the water at the dam. The gantry crane was buzzing with activity. "We'd never get near it," he said.

"That's your call," Barnard said. "I'm just letting you know the odds."

Chisnall considered that, then keyed his comm. "Wilton, what armaments can you see on that big crane?"

The gantry crane was a massive square platform on four stout legs. It moved on heavy-gauge railway tracks to open and close each of the flat bulkhead panels, behind which sat the curved main gates of the dam.

"There're at least eight heavy machine guns," Wilton said,

examining the gantry crane through binoculars. "One on each corner and one in the middle of each side."

"What else?" Chisnall asked.

"Not much that I can see."

"So make a guess."

"Rockets, that's what I'd do. SAMs, corkscrews. I'd stack that platform with everything I could lay my hands on."

"How would you attack it?" Chisnall asked.

Wilton hesitated. "To get near it, you have to travel along the road on top of the dam. That's one long road with no cover in either direction. They'd have a perfect field of fire, with a great height advantage. Then you'd have to assault the platform up those staircases." A metal staircase zigzagged up each of the legs. "I don't think it's possible, LT, unless . . ."

"Unless what?" Chisnall asked.

"You remember what they taught us in judo?"

"What?"

"To take down a big guy, take out his legs," Wilton said.

Chisnall switched his comm to the command channel. "Task Force Actual, this is Angel One."

"Clear copy, Angel One."

"I need to talk to Colonel Fairbrother, over."

"This better be important, Angel One."

"It is, Task Force Actual."

Fairbrother came on the line a minute later. He sounded breathless and there was constant gunfire in the background. "What have you got, Chisnall?"

"Colonel, we believe we can breach the dam gates. If it works, it will flood and destroy the Lowood plant."

"What about those generators?"

"Sir, it is my belief that blowing the generators would not achieve the mission objective. The fuel plant would continue to operate."

"Can you do both?" Fairbrother asked.

"No. We don't have enough C4."

The line went dead. Chisnall waited.

"Chisnall, you better be right. Do you know what's riding on this?"

"Sir, yes, I think I do."

"The fate of the human race is riding on this, Chisnall. Do you get that? Do you really get what that means? If we can't get through to the fuel plant, then the existence of the human race on this planet is going to depend on whether Lieutenant Ryan Bloody Chisnall made the right bloody decision."

"I understand that, sir."

Fairbrother went silent again, although the line stayed open this time. Chisnall could hear explosions and shooting through the earpiece. It sounded close.

"It rather looks like we're out of options," Fairbrother said. "If we can't get in, we'll get clear. I will call you when the task force is at a safe distance."

"Take the Lowood Hills Road, get as high as you can."

"I can read a bloody map, Lieutenant."

The channel clicked off. "They're having a bad time of it," Chisnall said.

"You think they make it through?" Monster asked.

"I think we'd better be ready," Chisnall said. "In case they don't."

"You'd better pray that this works," the Tsar said. "In case they don't."

Chisnall nodded but said nothing. His decision was made.

Monster and the Tsar had removed the heavy machine gun from the boat and were welding the tripod stand onto the front tray of one of the quad bikes. Price and Barnard had jury-rigged three buoys using rope they found in a storeroom, large plastic water containers that they emptied and lashed together in pairs, and more of the water containers, filled with dirt, to act as anchors.

"So some suicidal maniac has to take one of these right up to the dam gates," Price said. "Who's going to volunteer for that job?"

"I am," Chisnall said.

24. BUOYS WITH BOMBS

[1050 hours local time]
[Lake Wivenhoe, New Bzadia]

"NOW?" PRICE ASKED. SHE FELT VULNERABLE AND EXposed in a small open boat in the middle of the lake.

"Not yet," Barnard said.

The boat wallowed in the water under the weight of three heavy fuel cells, plus the buoy anchors. Watchful eyes from the dam followed them as they motored to the specified coordinates.

"That's it," Barnard said, her eyes never leaving the GPS readout on her wrist computer. She idled the engine of the boat, maintaining the position, while Price heaved the anchor over the side. The rope slithered over the gunnels of the boat but stopped with a jerk as the rope tightened on the bomb they had created using a fuel cell and a C4 satchel.

Price armed the satchel and connected an aerial wire, then placed the makeshift buoy in the water before rolling the fuel cell over the side of the boat. More rope snaked out over the gunnels and Price let the aerial wire run through her fingers to make sure it did not get damaged. The rope disappeared, as did the buoy for a second, just long enough for Price to wonder if the combined weight of the bomb and the anchor was too much—but then it bobbed back to the surface. She fastened the end of the wire to the buoy with duct tape, and Barnard let the boat drift away from the location before gunning the motor and turning toward the next GPS position.

Price looked over at the dam, and the crane that rose above it. They were well out of range, but that didn't make her feel any more comfortable. Barnard noticed her looking.

"You and Monster are going to hold C4 satchels and ride right up to that crane?" Barnard asked.

Price shrugged. "You wanna swap places?"

"Uh-uh, I still have a vague hope of getting out of here alive," Barnard said, checking their position against her GPS screen. "Why'd you volunteer for it?"

"Someone had to do it," Price said.

"And like Wilton said, you don't want to let your buddies down?"

"Pretty stupid, huh," Price said.

"And Monster? He's pretty stupid too?"

"Monster is a lot smarter than he acts," Price said. "But he hides it well."

"I know," Barnard said. "He can't hide it from me."

Price thought of the way that Barnard's eyes burned into people when she was talking to them, and thought that was probably true. "I think he does it to fool people so they underestimate him," she said.

"What about all that wacky New Age spiritual stuff?" Barnard asked. "All part of the disguise?"

"Don't know," Price said. "That started after Uluru. It changed him a bit, I think. We've all changed since Uluru. Well, maybe not Wilton."

"You like him, don't you?" Barnard said.

"Wilton?"

"Monster."

"What do you mean?" Price asked, suddenly off balance.

"Like, fancy, adore, love," Barnard said, correcting her steering by half a degree. "Soul mates. Two hearts beating as one. You can't wait for this war to be over so you can settle down with him in some quaint little Monster house and raise cute little Monster kids."

"I thought you said there was no such thing as love," Price said.

"Maybe I was just being cynical," Barnard said. "Does he feel the same way?"

Price trailed a hand in the water beside the boat, liking the feeling of the lake rushing through her fingers. Liking the simplicity of it.

"I . . . think so," she said after a while.

"You don't know?"

"We went out for a while back at camp. After Uluru."

"And?"

"I broke it off."

"Why?"

"What's the point?" Price asked. "One or the other or both of us are not going to survive this war."

"The point is," Barnard said, slowing the engine and circling around to zero in on the next position, "that one or the other or both of you are not going to survive this war."

Price opened her mouth to protest, but then shut it again. After a moment she said, "You're a very smart person."

"I know," Barnard said.

"That's not what I meant," Price said.

"I know," Barnard said.

"I didn't like you much at first," Price said. "But you're kinda cool."

"Don't waste it," Barnard said.

"Waste what?"

"Whatever time you two might have."

The rotorcraft came in low and fast, landing almost a mile southwest of the dam with a thud that sent spikes of pain up Yozi's leg. Even before the craft had fully touched down, they were leaping off onto springy coils of grass. A gravel slope rose up out of the farmland above them, the huge earth embankment of the dam. The mighty gates stood between giant concrete pillars. If Yozi had had his way, they would have landed right on the dam itself, but the pilot had refused, worried about the humans' deadly javelin missiles.

Alizza was in the lead, but Yozi was at his heels, and the other eighteen members of the squad were right behind them.

25. THE DAM

[1130 hours local time]
[Lake Wivenhoe, New Bzadia]

THE BATTLE FOR THE WIVENHOE DAM BEGAN AT 11:30 hours.

It started in a haze of white as the Angels launched smoke grenade after smoke grenade from the eastern road, then slipped through the trees to get as close as possible to the dam before launching their assault.

The breeze was in their favor—westerly, carrying the smoke across the top of the dam, but light, so the smoke did not disperse too quickly. To the Bzadians up on the ramparts of the giant gantry crane, the smoke must have been unsettling. Things were happening down in the haze below them but they did not know what, or where, to shoot. Occasional single coil-gun shots and bursts of machine-gun fire sounded. Shooting at shadows.

The noise of motorcycle engines reverberated through the haze. Two or three of them at least, but the Bzadians could not know that was just to confuse them, to disguise the sound of the one bike that mattered, the quad bike on which Price and Monster waited.

On the waters of the lake, well out of range of the guns on the gantry, Chisnall also waited, alone in the boat, the engine idling, the bows settled in the water. If ever he had to depend on his team, it was now. If they couldn't take out the defenses on the gantry crane, he wouldn't make it within a hundred meters of the dam. He looked at the bomb balanced in the front of the craft and at the detonator clipped to his thigh.

"Do it," he said, barely more than a murmur.

The engines of all the bikes roared, and now Price and Monster were moving—Price driving, Monster carrying one of the C4 satchels, the other clipped to the handlebars. One stray bullet and they would be a red smear along the road. The smoke was patchy but thick in parts, and Price kept right to the center of the concrete road, judging her distance from the tracks of the crane to the left and right, visible for just a few meters in front of her.

Now the Angels behind them opened up, their guns pre-sighted on the ramparts of the gantry before the smoke had started. The heavy machine gun jury-rigged onto the front of the other quad bike began a heavy stutter. The Angels' coil-guns added to the cacophony blazing out at the high platform.

The Bzadians began to respond, firing blindly into the smoke below them. Price corrected her course slightly and gave the quad bike more gas. The front lifted and the bike surged ahead.

A corkscrew rocket came spiraling out of the smoke, impacting on the guardrail in front of them with a roar and a scream of twisted metal. Shrapnel clattered off Price's visor and armor as she drove through the residue of the explosion.

More explosions now, to the left and the right, heated rushing air blasting around them. The sound of bullets fizzed through the air.

They were at the legs of the crane and Price was braking, hard. Monster rolled off the back with one of the satchels and she accelerated away without ever actually stopping.

The other leg of the gantry loomed, a dark tower, and she skidded the quad bike to a halt. Bullets were ricocheting all around as the Bzadians realized what was happening.

There was no time for anything fancy. She hit the button to start the timer and tossed the satchel down by the leg of the beast. Then she was gunning the bike again, back to the first leg, where Monster was waiting.

He swung himself onto the back and they were racing back to the east side of the dam, to safety.

The rocket that got them was a fluke, the soldier above firing blind. It corkscrewed into the ground about two meters away, blasting Price off the bike and sending it spinning up through the air and out over the edge of the dam. Only a safety fence saved her as she slid across the roadway, dazed and half-blinded, her ears ringing with a constant high-pitched whistle.

Monster was nowhere to be seen, over the edge of the dam perhaps or a bloodied, shredded body lying somewhere on the roadway.

Seconds slid by, although time meant nothing to her. It was the shape of the Bzadian soldiers appearing through the smoke that finally spurred her into action. Rolling back onto her hands and knees and crawling forward, she found her way blocked by combat boots. Black-suited soldiers were standing over her, their coil-guns aimed at her head. Such was the pain and the confusion in her head that it was only then, when she stopped, certain that this was the end, that she noticed her leg. It was gone. Her right leg below the knee was missing and yet somehow she had crawled on the stump, leaving a bloody trail along the concrete behind her.

Price shut her eyes and, even as she did, the insides of her eyelids flashed brilliant red as a sheet of white lightning lit the scene like a flash photograph. Then came the rush of burning air over the top of her. The C4 on the legs of the crane. Had she been standing, she would have been blasted off her feet by a thump of superheated air, but lying on the roadway she was spared most of the explosion.

The Bzadians disappeared, debris on the wind, some flying out over the edge of the dam.

And above her, the gantry crane danced a crazy dance on broken legs as it swayed back and forth, flapping and flopping before toppling, in a scream of awful twisted metal, out over the gates of the dam and into the slipway below.

Monster was gone. Amid the pain and the confusion and the shock, that fact finally registered in her brain. And with it came a pain more searing than any ravages of skin, bone, or flesh. Weeping uncontrollably now, she unclipped her utility belt and pulled it tightly around the stump of her leg, a make-shift tourniquet, and probably too little, too late.

A dark shape rose up out of the rubble and strode toward her. For a moment, Price hoped against hope that it was Monster, that somehow he had survived the blast, but even through eyes blurred with tears, she knew that this shape was wrong. It was too tall, the shoulders not broad enough. It drew closer and finally she recognized his uneven teeth. A grotesque leering thing, an ugly creature from an ugly species. His name, Price remembered dimly through the fog in her brain, was Alizza.

Chisnall was moving, skipping across the surface of the water, as fast as the boat would go. Even before the twin explosions that had taken down the gantry and its deadly weaponry, he had been racing full throttle toward the dam. Now he slowed the boat as he moved into the funnel, the twin arms of concrete that stretched out from the dam gates.

He spun the boat around to bleed off speed, then let it coast up to the massive metal bulkhead gates. Tall flat sheets of solid metal, impossibly thick, the tops of them rising out of the water. It was hard to imagine an explosive even denting such behemoths.

He chose the center gate and pulled the boat up alongside it, rolling the heavy fuel cell over the side, ignoring the pain from his broken rib. The fuel cell sank so rapidly that the flying rope almost caught his foot, and he just had time to flip the buoy out into the water before the rope snatched it from his grasp.

He gunned the engine, arcing around in a spray of white water and heading for the wide-open water of the lake.

He hoped the others were all right, but there was no time to even think about that. They had done their job; now it was time for him to do his.

From the top of the dam, Yozi watched the boat surging away. A flash of a face and he knew it was Chizna at the tiller. There had to be a reason for that, and staring down the face of the dam gates he saw it. Two plastic bottles full of air, bobbing against the gates.

An explosive.

Yozi raised himself up and yelled directions to the remains of his squad; the others had been decimated by the explosions that had taken down the gantry.

Those who could raced to the edge of the dam and began to lay down fire at the retreating boat.

Yozi stripped off his weapon and his heavy armor, climbed

up onto the railing, and jumped off, feetfirst, into the rippling waters below.

Alizza had no weapon. It had been snatched from his arms by the claws of the explosion. His armor was shattered; his visor was gone. He took off the remains of his helmet as he advanced on Price and threw it to the ground.

She pushed herself upward, knowing that even in the best of shape she was no match for this creature, and right now she could offer little more than a token resistance.

Alizza reached down for her. She kicked at him with her one leg, momentarily breaking his grip, suddenly sure what he was doing. So simple. So efficient. So brutal. He was going to hurl her off the side of the dam.

She kicked and fought, but her muscles were loose and he was too strong. He lifted her up but abruptly let her go again and staggered backward into a swirl of smoke.

"Leave her alone," a voice said, and Monster was there.

Chisnall spun the boat around as he heard the splash and saw a Bzadian emerge, coughing and spluttering, in the water at the base of the dam. Something looked familiar about the face of the soldier.

Yozi!

He gunned the boat, racing back to the dam, desperate to stop Yozi before he could disable the bomb.

Bullets kicked up the water before him, making miniature waterspouts. More clanged off the cowling of the motor. Chisnall was forced to swing away again, racing out of range as the water behind him erupted with gunfire.

In the water, Yozi began to swim toward the buoy.

Alizza stood up, grinning his terrible gap-toothed smile, actually pleased, Price thought, to see Monster again.

That was when she noticed the blood pouring from cuts in Monster's shoulders and arms, and the way he held his right hand. The explosion had not left him unscathed.

Alizza advanced toward him, still grinning. "The last time we met," he said, "you had the advantage of surprise."

Monster did not smile back. "The last time we met, I held no anger for you," he said.

"This time you are angry?" Alizza looked from Monster to Price, then back again. "Ah, so this is your paired female."

Monster flared his nostrils but said nothing. He did not deny it.

Price scrabbled for the sidearm that should have been in her leg holster, but it was gone. So was the holster, torn away by the blast or the slide along the roadway. So was most of the leg.

"The last time we met," Monster said, "it was within my power to kill you, and I chose not to."

"The last time we met"—Alizza grinned—"I did not have a knife."

He reached to his belt and withdrew a bzuntu, a jagged war knife, which he raised and tossed from hand to hand expertly.

"Everything will be as it should be," Monster said.

"On that we both agree," Alizza said.

Again Chisnall tried to maneuver back to the dam, this time weaving the boat from side to side, trying to throw the Bzadian gunners off their aim. There was no way. Bullets stitched a line of holes across the gunnels and he spun the boat around, heading back out of range.

Yozi reached the makeshift buoy. He clutched at the nearest of the bottles bobbing on the surface of the water. He put his head under the water briefly.

Chisnall picked up the detonator.

He flicked his comm onto the command channel.

"Task Force Actual, immediate interrogative. What is your status?"

Desperate cries and shouts came amid heavy fighting on the other end before a breathless voice came on. The radio cut in and out, giving him only a few words at a time.

"Can't get through . . . retreating . . ."

"Task Force Actual!" Chisnall yelled. "Are you clear?"

"Negative, Angel One . . . retreating . . . Give us fifteen minutes."

Yozi's head came up again and flicked around, looking directly at Chisnall.

"Fifteen minutes, Angel One. How copy?"

“Solid copy, Task Force Actual,” Chisnall said. He copied them all right. The problem was he didn’t have fifteen minutes.

“Gotta blow it, Chisnall.” The Tsar’s voice came on the comm. “You may not get another chance.”

“LT, the entire task force is trapped in that valley,” Wilton said.

“It’s not about the task force,” the Tsar said. “It’s about the human race.”

“Barnard?” Chisnall cried out desperately.

“It’s your decision, Ryan,” Barnard said.

“I can’t . . . ,” Chisnall said.

Yozi’s feet kicked up into the air as he dived below the surface of the water.

Monster was kneeling over her, saying soothing things, although Price could not make out the words. The weeping had stopped now. She was shivering, from shock and fear, but his presence made it seem that things would be all right, that there was still hope.

He held a knife, a jagged bzuntu blade, and it was dripping with blood. She saw him toss it over the side of the dam.

He was examining what remained of her leg now—she sensed that rather than saw it—and there was a feeling of pressure, through the pain. Then his arms were around her, picking her up, and she had just enough strength left to nestle her head into his shoulder. She felt warm and safe as the great darkness drifted over her and the pain floated away. Price smiled, because Monster was right—everything would turn out exactly the way it was supposed to be.

Yozi had been underwater for only a few seconds, but that was all it would take. If he followed the rope down to the bomb, it would take him just a few seconds to disarm it or detach the C4 from the fuel cell.

Chisnall flicked off the detonator safety catch. There was no choice. There never had been a choice. He pressed the switch that would begin the detonation sequence.

A deafening silence spread across the lake.

Chisnall looked at the switch, fighting the urge to press it again. That would do nothing. The sequence had started, but the charge by the gates of the dam had not detonated. The explosion the professors had said was necessary for the plan to succeed.

As he watched, Yozi surfaced, clutching the aerial wire. In the end it had been simple for him. He had simply removed the aerial from the satchel. There was no way for the radio signal to reach the bomb, ten meters underwater.

Yozi had won.

The Bzadians had won.

The human race was finished.

A roar from behind had Chisnall spinning around to see a waterspout rising into the air in the center of the lake. A second, more muted explosion closer to the dam resulted in nothing more than a rapid bubbling of the surface, like boiling water. The charge was too deep to create a waterspout. Of the third explosion he could see and hear nothing and could only assume that it had gone off.

His boat lurched into the air, rolled upward by a huge mound of water, traveling at high speed toward the dam. The boat plunged down into the trough behind the wave, only to climb skyward again on the next wave. The next wave was taller, closer to the surface, Chisnall realized, and therefore faster. He could see it closing in on the first wave; then he dropped into the chasm behind it and a moment later rode the third, highest and fastest of the waves, the boat almost launching itself upward, the propeller buzzing madly in thin air before the boat crashed back down for a third time.

"Look at the dam!" It was the Tsar's voice.

Chisnall twisted back. The small bay was dry. The water had receded, sucked out of the "funnel" by the approaching waves.

Chisnall was flung to the floor of the boat, his hand wrenched from the tiller of the outboard motor. He raised himself up in time to see the three waves arriving at the mouth of the funnel, converging into one. Then he saw Yozi.

The Bzadian was visible behind the rising curve of the water. As the water had receded, it had sucked him out with it. He was close enough for Chisnall to see the expression on his face. Confusion, turning to horror, then fading into resignation as the monster wave picked him up like a piece of flotsam.

The water was a living thing, a giant serpent, drawing back its head, then striking with unbelievable speed and ferocity at the dam, funneled by the concrete walls and the slope of the dam embankment.

Yozi disappeared, swallowed by hundreds of thousands of tons of water in that initial fist of destruction.

Chisnall realized that Barnard's Stanford pals had got it wrong. Very wrong. Although Chisnall had no way of knowing it, what the professors had failed to take into account was the reflection of the shock wave from the lake floor. Not one, but three reflections from three different explosions. Those reflected shock waves compounded the effect, amplifying the force of the water by more than three times.

The power of millions of tons of lake water clenched into a fist that punched at the gates was greater than anyone imagined. They had hoped for one gate to give way. What happened was way beyond anyone's expectations. The flat bulkhead gates gave way first, crumpling like aluminum foil. The huge curved main gates tried to resist, but it was futile. The ram of solid water smashed the massive triangular pivots from their concrete mounts and the gates became projectiles, popped out like peas from a peashooter over the slipway below.

Still the water was not satisfied. It exploded upward at the concrete wall and the roadway that ran across the top of the dam, pulverizing it, turning solid concrete into dust and crumbs.

Yozi's squad would have seen the water recede. Some of them might even have known what that meant, although it was doubtful. Bzadia was a desert planet, and a planet without oceans knows no beaches, no tsunamis. In any case there was no time. No time to run. Perhaps a little time to pray, but no more than to say *Azoh!* Then they were gone, tiny bits of flotsam and jetsam amid the great concrete boulders and turgid, spouting waters that poured over the gap in the dam where the gates used to be. But *poured* was the wrong word. *Pour* is something that water does from a tap. This was more akin to a fire hose, the water spurting, jetting, gushing in a horizontal line from the dam.

On the roadway to the left of the dam, Chisnall saw a figure emerge through the swirling smoke. Monster, battered and blackened, carrying a body in his arms. With a sinking feeling he knew it must be Price.

"Angel One, this is Task Force Actual. What the hell was that?" Fairbrother didn't wait for a reply. "Chisnall, we are *not* clear! I repeat, we are not clear!" The voice disappeared but came back on the channel before Chisnall could respond. "Oh my God . . ."

Then there was silence on the comm.

The full knowledge of what he had done hit Chisnall like a punch in the stomach.

"LT, get out of there!" Wilton yelled.

That was when he realized that he was going backward. Slowly but surely, the hungry gap in the wall of the dam was sucking him in.

He twisted the throttle and the boat surged ahead, but already the grip of the water was much stronger and the boat continued to swirl toward the hole in the dam. He jammed the throttle to full and for a few seconds he made progress before the remorseless flow again pulled him back.

"Steer to the side!" the Tsar yelled.

He did, but it was a halfhearted attempt. The rapid gurgling rush of water out through the broken dam sucked him in; the hunger of the beast for the one who had set it free could not be denied.

He tried to get around the edge of one of the concrete arms, to escape the funnel that was channeling the waters, but then he thought of the faces of the soldiers, men and women, American, Canadian, German, and Russian, still trapped in the valley below. He saw Monster carrying Price's lifeless body along the top of the dam embankment.

An overwhelming tiredness came over him.

His hand slipped from the tiller. Immediately, the straining engine settled down to an idle.

Like a bubble in a bath, gurgling down the drain, Chisnall felt himself pulled faster and faster.

He shut his eyes.

He waited.

Barnard watched in horror as the boat, now merely a toy amid the raging waters of the lake, was sucked toward the hole in the dam.

"Chisnall!" she screamed, but he could never have heard her, even on the comm, above the roaring of the water.

The boat spun in a small circle for a moment, caught in an eddy, then whirled out and hurtled over the side of the dam, disappearing into a torrent of water moving with such power and speed that it seemed like solid concrete.

A few scraps of debris that might once have been part of the boat appeared but were quickly sucked back in by the greedy maw of the water.

"Chisnall," Barnard said again, but there was no longer any urgency in her voice.

26. THE FLOOD

AT THE ACOG COMMAND CENTER IN THE BASEMENT OF the Pentagon, General Elisabeth Iniguez, commandant of the US Marine Corp and the instigator of Operation Magnum, watched the incoming satellite feeds with horror.

General Harry Whitehead stepped up beside her and put his hand on her shoulder.

The high-resolution satellite imagery showed clearly the bursting of the gates at the Wivenhoe Dam and the resulting destruction.

The waters scythed and twisted through the countryside, creating a turbulent maelstrom that ate everything in its path. It sucked trees right out of the ground. It swept up boulders that hadn't moved in thousands of years and hurled them like skipping stones. The river had no hope of containing the thunderous waters in its slender banks. The waters arced into the air in great long geysers before spreading out across the flat farmland.

That was merely an illusion. The incredible energy contained in the water had been spread but not diminished, and it reached the fuel plant at 11:43 hours with ferocious anger.

The vast concrete bunkers, which could have withstood direct hits from tomahawk missiles, shuddered under the barrage, water spraying into the air as the fury of the dam vented itself against the round Bzadian buildings.

Massive oak trees, wrenched out by their roots, battered at the concrete, while the water clawed and dug at the very foundations they rested on.

The first building to give way was a fuel laboratory at the northern end of the complex. The force of the water had brushed the high double fences protecting the plant aside and the chain-link metal wrapped itself around two of the buildings. Log after log slammed into the fence, trapped until a huge boulder rammed into the front of the building, smashing the wall, and the concrete roof of the building began to lift. The waters punched underneath, lifting the immense slab into the air like a toy boat floating on a stream and slamming it down onto the building behind it. That structure, a piping station, collapsed as the two slabs destroyed each other, chunks of broken concrete thrust along in the hurricane of water and smashing into the buildings behind them.

Over and around them the floodwaters spewed and spat logs, boulders, and broken chunks of concrete.

At 11:53 hours a mass of concrete, metal, and wood pummeled down on the largest building at the southern end of the plant. It was a warehouse, packed with fuel cells, waiting for distribution to the Chukchi Peninsula.

The wall collapsed and the unstoppable force poured inside.

Fuel cells, smashed against each other with incredible speed and force, exploded.

The explosion rippled through the cells in a chain reaction. One moment there was a wall of water tearing toward the soldiers of the task force; the next moment the sun came out.

General Iniguez flinched as the satellite imagery completely whited out for a second. When the pictures resumed, there was no visibility at all, just a massive cloud covering the scene. It was a huge cloud of steam, water vaporized by the heat of the explosion. It obscured the area for the next twenty minutes.

The blast was a momentary pause; then the waters rushed back in to fill the vacuum, even more viciously this time, as if angered. Bzadian forces in the area were obliterated. Any who survived the initial shock wave had no chance against the murderous hunger of the waters. On the southern side of the town, the ACOG joint task force fared no better. Stunned by the initial shock wave, they had no protection against the sudden ocean that appeared where a river had been.

Twelve thousand fully armed combat soldiers started the operation.

There were no survivors.

27. ANGELS

[1200 hours local time]
[Lake Wivenhoe, New Bzadia]

BARNARD WATCHED AS MONSTER CARRIED THE MANGLED body down from the dam wall. He laid Price on the back tray of the quad bike and strapped her in place. The lower half of one of her legs was missing, and a makeshift tourniquet was still tightly strapped above the knee.

Wilton was nearby, his hands by his sides, his coil-gun still held loosely in one hand. He was looking in the other direction. Refusing to see.

The Tsar sat on the ground, his head in his hands.

Monster's eyes met Barnard's. "Chisnall?"

Barnard shook her head.

Monster's face was emotionless. He threw a leg across the bike and pressed the starter, which whined and spat before roaring into life.

Barnard moved over and put a hand on his arm. "She really liked you, you know," she said.

"We must move north," Monster said. "Try to get to extraction point."

He kicked the bike into gear.

"I think she would have wanted you to know that," Barnard said.

"Price is tough son of britches." Monster pointed backward with a thumb. "Is not dead yet."

A voice came from the back of the bike. "Yes, I bloody am."

END NOTE

THE ANGELS CAME HOME.

The escape of the Angel Team over the weeks that followed Operation Magnum is the stuff of legend, and the team's use of SERE (Survive, Evade, Resist, Extract) training to avoid being captured by Bzadian forces is a textbook case of survival behind enemy lines. It is still studied in military schools all over the world.

Eight days after Operation Magnum, the remaining members of Recon Team Angel reached the coast of Australia and activated an emergency beacon. They were picked up by the USS *Morgan Stanley* on January 10 and were back at Fort Carson less than a week after that.

The survival of Sergeant Trianne Price, despite the loss of a leg, is regarded as something of a modern miracle, but in reality is a tribute to her toughness, determination, and the constant medical care provided by Specialist Janos (Monster) Panyoczki.

Opinion on Operation Magnum has shifted over time. Most historians now regard it as a military success, a noble sacrifice that gave the Free Territories enough time to rebuild and reinforce their defenses in preparation for the coming Ice War. It was a turning point in the Bzadian War.

The instigator of the operation, General Elisabeth Iniguez, saw things differently. She resigned as the commandant of the US Marine Corps immediately after Operation Magnum.

The court-martial of the Angel Team also caused bitter debate on both sides, but all surviving members were exonerated of any wrongdoing. Still, there was intense pressure from the public to disband the team. Already uncomfortable with the concept of the Angels, it took a negative view of the operation, with its high cost of human lives.

Under such public pressure, ACOG military commanders had no choice.

On March 1, 2032, the Recon Team Angel and Recon Team Demon programs were officially shut down.

Unofficially? That is a different story.

EPILOGUE

HE TRIED TO OPEN HIS EYES BUT COULD NOT. WHEREVER he was, it was dark. No light filtered through his eyelids.

He was wet and cold. Cautiously raising an arm, he was pleasantly surprised to find that he could. He moved his hand to his face, feeling around his eyes and touching a soft, gelatinous substance. He wiped away as much as he could, although mainly he seemed to succeed in smearing it around his face. By wiping his hand on his uniform, he was able to clear some of the mud from his eyes, and he opened one of them to reveal waving palm trees above, framed by a blue, blue sky.

Hallucinating or dreaming? Neither turned out to be true. He looked to the left and the right and realized that he was lying on the bank of the river, in a pool of mud. His body was stuck firmly, but his legs still seemed to be in the water. He could not feel them, but he could see his feet, rocking back and forth with the movement of the water.

He tried to move his legs, to push himself farther out of the water, but they did not respond.

He touched the side of his body with his hand, tenderly pressing on his ribs, and was strangely relieved by the agonizing pain that resulted. His stomach area seemed intact. His hips were there but felt dead, as though he were touching the hips of someone else. His legs felt the same. Everything below his waist was like rubber. Like touching a dead body. There were concerned voices now, faces above him, and feet splashing down into the mud beside him. They were Bzadian faces and he tried to hold on to the thought, *Don't speak English.* He was in Bzadian uniform. He looked Bzadian. But one word in English would give it all away.

Hands were pulling at him, trying to lift him up out of the mud, and a searing pain overwhelmed his brain; then everything faded once again to black.

The doctor entered holding a full-body holographic X-ray. She spun it around a few times in midair, zooming in and out of various bones, frowning. She smiled at him when she saw he was watching.

Her dark hair was cut in a short bob style that the aliens called a sierfruit, because it resembled the small Bzadian fruit. She was older, but not old, Chisnall thought. It was difficult to tell the age of the aliens, as their faces did not crease and line as easily as human faces. Her smile seemed genuine, though, and well used, although that might have been part of her job description rather than part of her personality.

She was tall, almost certainly a bobble-head, as humans called that particular Bzadian race.

Yozi had been a bobble-head. He was dead now.

He was the enemy, but in many ways Chisnall had felt a kinship for him. He had admired Yozi's concern for the troops in his squad. He had envied his bravery, diving into the waters of the lake for a bomb that could have exploded at any time.

Chisnall was silent, and the doctor said nothing, as if waiting for him to speak, which seemed unusual, considering the circumstances.

"Will I walk again?" Chisnall asked after a while.

She seemed surprised by the question. She nodded, as if it was unnecessary. "I think so. We'll have to rebuild part of your spinal cord, but it shouldn't be a problem."

Her head bobbled slightly as she spoke, confirming Chisnall's guess.

She moved across to the door and closed it, then returned and sat on a chair next to the bed, idly spinning the hologram around.

"Of course, it would be easier if you were Bzadian," she said.

The words hung like ice in the air.

"You know," Chisnall said.

"How could I not?" the doctor said. "The changes are

superficial only. I'd estimate that you are about seventeen years old. From one of the Caucasian races."

Chisnall shut his eyes and rested his head back on the roll of soft rubber that the Bzadians used as a pillow. "Close enough," he said.

After another long silence she said, "Some kind of spy, I presume."

"A soldier," Chisnall said. "Not a spy."

Not that it mattered. They would execute him either way, with as much compunction as he would have swatting a troublesome mosquito.

"A soldier. Of course," she said. "But still a human."

Chisnall shrugged.

There was a long silence.

"Well, I suppose for now that had better remain our little secret," she said, and stood up.

Chisnall started to speak, but the doctor pressed her finger to her lips.

She turned back briefly as she reached the door. "Many died up at Lowood. Both humans and Bzadians. Yet somehow you were washed miles downstream and survived." She looked at him, evaluating him. "You were very lucky," she said; then she was gone and he was alone.

Lucky? he thought. *Maybe. But that luck seems to be rapidly running out.*

GLOSSARY

Everything about the Allied Combined Operations Group (ACOG) was a mishmash of different human cultures: tactics, weapons, languages, vehicles, and especially terminology. The success of many missions depended on troops from diverse nations being able to understand all communications instantly and thoroughly. The establishment of a Standardized Military Terminology and Phonetic Alphabet (SMTPA) was a key factor in assisting this communication, combining existing terminology from many of the countries involved in ACOG. For ease of understanding, here is a short glossary of some of the SMTPA terms, phonetic shortcuts, and equipment used in this book.

ACOG: Allied Combined Operations Group

Cal: caliber (of weapon)

Clear copy: "Your transmission is clear."

Coil-gun: weapon using magnetic coils to propel a projectile

Comm: personal radio communicator

DPV: driver propulsion vehicle

EV (Echo Victor): exit vehicle

Eyes on: to have sight of

Fast mover: fixed-wing aircraft such as a jet fighter

FFC: forward fire control

GPS: global positioning system

How copy: "Is my transmission clear?"

Klick: kilometer

LOT: lock-out trunk

LT: lieutenant

Mike: minute

MPC: marine personnel carrier

NV goggles: night-vision goggles

Oscar Kilo: okay

Oscar Mike: on the move

PFC: private first class

Puke: military slang for a Bzadian

Rotorcraft: helicopter with internal rotor blades at the base of the craft

RPG: rocket-propelled grenade

Slow mover: rotary-wing aircraft such as a helicopter or rotorcraft

SONRAD: sonar/radar

Spec: specialist

Three, six, etc.: direction given as per a clock face

Note on Pronunciation

There is no equivalent in English for the buzzing sound that is a common feature of most Bzadian languages. As per convention, this sound is represented, where required, with the letter z.

Note on Bzadian Army Ranks

The ranking system and unit structure of the Bzadian Army are markedly different from those of most Earth forces. Many ranks have no equivalent in human terms, and the organization of units is different. For simplicity and ease of understanding, the closest human rank has been used when referring to Bzadian Army ranks, and Bzadian unit names have been expressed in human terms.

Congratulations

The following people won the grand prize in my school competitions and have all had a character named after them in this book:

Retha Barnard
Albany Junior High School, Auckland, New Zealand

Holly Brogan
St. Cuthbert's College, Auckland, New Zealand

Ryan Chisnall
Belmont Intermediate, Auckland, New Zealand

Liam Fairbrother
Masterton Intermediate, Masterton, New Zealand

Elisabeth Iniguez

Vista Del Valle Elementary School, Los Angeles, USA

Janos Panyoczki

Kaiwaka School, Kaiwaka, New Zealand

Trianne Price

Woodcrest State College, Queensland, Australia

Hayden Wall

Padua College, Queensland, Australia

Harry Whitehead

Waimea College, Richmond, New Zealand

Blake Wilton

Orewa College, Orewa, New Zealand

ABOUT THE AUTHOR

BRIAN FALKNER, a native New Zealander, now lives in sunny Queensland, Australia. His keen interest in military history inspired the futuristic "history" of the Recon Team Angel books. Find him online at brianfalkner.com.